When Izzy gets a killer dress for her birthday, she isn't expecting to accessorize it with murder...

It's 1958 in the cozy coastal town of Twin Oaks and amateur sleuth Isabelle Walsh is armed with a fresh perspective, two years after tragedy strikes. The first stop on her journey back to joy is the best little dress shop in town—introduced to her by best friend and fashion fiend, Ava Russell.

Izzy falls in love with the store and its style. So, when the boutique is marred by murder, Izzy wants to help. But with more suspects to choose from than a spring collection, she isn't sure where to start.

Can Izzy unravel the twisted truth or will she become the victim of a deadly trend? Find out in the third book in the Izzy Walsh Mystery Series!

Praise for the Izzy Walsh Mystery Series

"Wonderful character development and dialogue. Thoroughly enjoyed it!!" ~ *Liz*

"Such a fun summer read! The characters are a delight and the story moves along at a rapid-fire pace to really keep the reader engaged. Look forward to seeing more from this series." ~ *DHC*

"Don't miss this cozy, page turning mystery with a smart list of characters and technicolor descriptions of the time period. A great choice for a relaxing vacation or a splurge for a rainy day" ~ *Zari Reede*

ACKNOWLEDGMENTS

A big thank you to Kerrin Hands and Black Opal Books—without your hard work and vision, my book wouldn't exist.

Thank you to Averyl, Mom, and Dad for your constant love and support. It means the world.

Troy, you always cheer me on and support me every day. I am so lucky to have you as my husband.

To the best aunt/editor, Stella. You are amazing!

To Scarlett and Remy, I am so grateful to be your mom. I love you always.

The
Girls Dressed
for Murder

AN IZZY WALSH MYSTERY

Lynn McPherson

A Black Opal Books Publication

Nita,
Thanks for all your support!
Happy reading!! *Lynn*

GENRE: HISTORICAL MYSTERY

This is a work of fiction. Names, places, characters and incidents are either the product of the author's imagination or are used fictitiously, and any resemblance to any actual persons, living or dead, businesses, organizations, events or locales is entirely coincidental. All trademarks, service marks, registered trademarks, and registered service marks are the property of their respective owners and are used herein for identification purposes only. The publisher does not have any control over or assume any responsibility for author or third-party websites or their contents.

*For Rita and Louise—the best moms, friends,
and role models I could ever wish for.*

Chapter 1

Time goes by faster as we age. I read that somewhere, but it never made any sense—until recently. My upcoming birthday seemed to be approaching much more quickly than my last one had. Dammit. *How was that possible?* Looking around the empty house, I wondered if it was simply a matter of having too much time to think. I no longer basked in the peaceful quiet my house provided. I missed the loud chaos—something I never thought I could years back. Now that my kids were teenagers, they weren't around as much to cause a ruckus. I needed to have a talk with them. Their growing interests outside of the home were starting to make me think about unpleasant things like aging. Summer camp was proving especially difficult in this regard. It was hard to believe my kids had grown to be so independent. I looked forward to their return already, and they had only been gone four days. Another week and a half was sure to send me to the brink. Perhaps it was time to consider canine companionship.

It had been four years since Frank's passing. They say everyone deals with grief differently. I hid away and clutched at the solace my children provided by their very existence. It took a long time to unclench that grip. At the beginning, it was as if I was holding on for my own dear life. But slowly it released as the range of emotions I experienced became less intense—less raw. Joy began to trickle back into my life, and I knew that was it. Besides, forty was only a few years away. And, as my best friend Ava had begun to remind me, I was still here. It was time to get on with life. Frank would be forever with me in my heart and soul, and that comforted me beyond words. I took a big swig of coffee, allowed myself to sit quietly with my tidal grief, then shook my head to rid it of the approaching sadness I felt creeping in when I indulged too long.

I looked out the window onto my empty suburban crescent and changed my focus onto my immediate circumstance. I was up, dressed, and styled at an indecently early hour on account of my aforementioned oldest, dearest, and most exasperating best friend. And...she was late. Rarely could Ava Russell make it anywhere on time. But she was due to be here fifteen minutes ago, and that was allowing for her usual lateness. Considering the brunette beauty only had to get her long legs about three blocks from her front door to mine, I could feel the little patience I had slowly oozing out of my body.

I tried to force my furrowed brow to smooth with my index finger, silently cursing Ava for adding to the accelerating aging process by inciting this early onset of wrinkles—the idea of which was first prompted by her regular commentary of what she called my overly expressive expressions. Luckily, my frown soon lifted as I spotted my kindred spirit making her way down the street. As she came closer into view, my nose pressed against the window like a magnet to metal in an attempt to get a better look. Something was up—my usually proud and polished companion had transformed from a perfect rose to a wilted weed. The mystery was solved as I spotted Ava's footwear. Sky-high stilettos left no doubt as to why she was struggling to strut. I watched her pull each shoe off angrily and finish her walk in stocking feet.

A grin spread across my face as I opened the door. I attempted to calm it as Ava laboriously dragged herself into my living room and flopped onto the sofa. She wasn't able to acknowledge me at first, instead puffing out her breaths one after the other, as if having completed a marathon.

Her crumpled figure still held her beautiful black heels in one hand as she looked up at me warily through her thick black mascara.

She pursed her lips. "Water," she whispered.

I nodded in assent and fetched a tall glass filled to the brim. She lapped it up like a thirsty young pup might do after a jaunt at the park. Ava finished her drink and lay back, finally having the opportunity to catch her breath. She looked up at me and cringed. "What is so damned funny, Izzy?"

I felt my eyes widen and clasped at my chest innocently. "I am a picture of serenity. Calm and humorless."

I put my hand on her forehead to check her temperature sympathetically.

She playfully swatted it away. "You think I can't see that stifled goofy smile? Your eyes are practically giggling right out of their sockets."

I gave up my attempt to deny it and allowed my grin to be free. "Fine, you've got my number. But honestly, Ava, what possessed you to select those particular shoes to walk over here? It doesn't require a lot of common sense to know stilettos are not a good choice for a stroll."

She sat back and let out a loud huff. "Yes, Izzy, I'm aware of that. But I paid a fortune for these. I assumed part of the cost was for the engineering of a more comfortable shoe. Boy, did I have that wrong."

Lesson learned. What Ava lacked in common sense she made up for in loyalty and fun. There was no need to say any more about her failings. "I am very impressed you walked here. I would've fallen in a ditch halfway, praying for you to come find me."

She nodded curtly in response then finished the few sips of water left in her glass. Ava had been trying out different forms of exercise after reading about some of her favorite Hollywood starlets' fitness routines. Over the last few weeks she'd gone through everything from tap dancing to hula hooping. Unfortunately, Ava had never been particularly athletic so her attempts led mostly to rolled ankles and broken vases.

When her ever-so-sensible husband pleaded with her to start with simpler activities for the sake of his wallet and her health, she complied. I doubt he foresaw an injury from the mutually agreed upon act of walking.

Luckily, Ava was a resilient woman so it didn't take her long to fully recover from any injury she sustained, including this one. To speed up her recovery, I brought out my ginger snap cookies that she loved.

Within a few minutes, she was ready to take on the day, all thoughts of the momentary setback forgotten. "I'm excited you're coming with me to Robin's Closet."

"Me, too. Wait—didn't the name change to Barbara's Closet?"

"Officially yes, but when Barbara bought the shop, she couldn't realistically expect people to call it that."

I frowned. "Why not? She's the new owner."

"Robin Manners brought New York fashion to our very own Twin Oaks. I think that fact alone should earn her name on the store, whether she abandoned it or not."

"Robin got married. That doesn't qualify as abandonment," I reminded her.

"I am well aware of the circumstances, of course. But you can't blame a girl for feeling the sting of such a loss. There was at least a year or two that the shop was no better than ordering straight out of a catalogue."

I peered down at my sensible white blouse and navy capris, purchased directly from the very pages of which she spoke. "That's what people do. Without having a big city department store in our charming coastal town, it's the normal way to purchase nice and respectable clothing. To be honest, I'm a little nervous going to Robin's and trying on something else. I have full confidence in catalogue wear. I'm not so confident straying elsewhere."

"Izzy Walsh, you need to loosen up a bit. Robin is brilliant and you'll love it."

"But what if I don't like anything? Will Barbara make me buy something anyway? You know she always gets her way."

"No need to worry," Ava said. "Barbara is there less and less these days. I guess owning her own shop has begun to lose its charm."

I wasn't surprised. "Since we were teenagers, she's had a hard time staying focused on anything for very long. She's gone from one thing to the next. She sees something she wants and she gets it. It's about getting her own way."

Ava stood up and walked back to the front door. She expertly slid back into her high heels and retrieved her kitten-framed polka-dotted black and white sunglasses from her snappy red handbag. "You're right. And with her father—and then her husband—indulging every whim, why would Barbara ever change? Must be nice. Now, let's go, slowpoke. They get their new shipments in on Thursdays, and I want to be first in line to see what came in. No dillydallying."

I followed her out the door like a shadow, not wanting to be responsible for someone beating Ava to the latest looks. It was the kind of thing she might never forgive me for—she had a list.

Ava strode confidently toward my car in her designer shoes as I got the keys from my purse. I bit my lip to prevent another grin at my friend's expense. The idea of her having a lack of understanding about indulgence was rather comical. I hadn't known Ava's husband to ever say no to her, either. But I wouldn't fault her for it. Ava was a loving wife and Bruce adored her. Luckily for both, he made enough money to happily support her passion for fashion.

More recently, I too, had become a fairly wealthy woman. Before Frank died, he had expanded his business—growing from one modest garage to a chain that included several successful mechanic shops. He was so busy working his tail off, he never had time to enjoy the fruits of his labor. Then again, I hadn't indulged in anything more than simple necessities since he passed, either. It looked like today that might change. With a little prodding from my kids to treat myself while they were away, I decided that a new dress would be nice for my birthday. I reluctantly agreed to accompany Ava to her favorite clothing boutique. I just hoped I wouldn't end up looking ridiculous. I didn't have the flair Ava did either, so what looked fabulous on her tall voluptuous figure, often looked silly on my much more petite frame.

Pushing all doubts aside, I donned my own kitten-framed black sunglasses, courtesy of Ava, and revved the engine of my little red convertible. I looked in the side mirror and rolled my eyes. Some battles I was simply destined to lose.

Chapter 2

Nothing in our idyllic coastal town was particularly far. Ten minutes would pretty much get you
from one side to the other. Lucky for us, if we
ever had the urge for some big-city fun, New York was
less than an hour's drive away. Not that we got there
much these days, but I liked the possibility nonetheless.

When we pulled up in front of the Main Street store,
I untied my scarf and half-heartedly tried to settle my un-
ruly raven locks. Sizing it up with my hands, I realized
the futility and flipped it behind my shoulder instead.
Ava took an extra minute to reapply her signature red
lipstick and shake out her unaffected shoulder-length
hair. I waited for her in front of the shop, admiring the
window display.

The small shop expertly used its street frontage to
show its stylish apparel and draw attention from passers-
by. At the moment, there were two mannequins in the
window scene. The first one faced forward and wore a
bold black-and-white full-skirted polka-dot dress, hold-

ing a pair of binoculars as if looking out at the pedestrians walking by. The second donned a subtler, yet equally stylish outfit—an expertly tailored red suit jacket paired with a matching pencil skirt, accessorized with an elegant hair wrap. She was standing sideways, leaning over as if whispering a secret into the ear of her curious inanimate friend, which happened to emphasize how complimentary the outfit was to the female form. With a crisp white backdrop, the scene was fun and artistic.

I didn't notice Ava creep up behind me. "That could be us," she whispered in my ear.

I grinned at the thought. "I wonder if they'd have that red number in my size."

Ava wiggled her finger at me. "We'll ask but don't you dare commit yourself too quickly, you eager beaver. After resisting my shopping requests for so long, there's no way we're going to go in there and simply buy the first thing we see."

Rats. "All right then, but it's a contender. You can't argue that."

She agreed and we went inside. The shop was just as splendid on the inside. We were greeted warmly by two ladies. Ava stopped to chat but I just smiled and wandered off, taking the opportunity to look around for a few minutes on my own. Little details demonstrated that great care and pride went into the shop's design. I was also pleased to find western-styled white swinging doors that led to a small but private change area. There were separate stalls for customers to try on apparel and a few chairs set up next to a little table adorned with a coffee percola-

tor and a Maxwell House coffee can. A dish of red can-
dies sat next to it and a stack of cups and saucers ready
for the taking. It was an inviting spot that allowed shop-
pers to take their time and enjoy themselves.

Ava called me to the front where she was still chatting. Her open, friendly manner put people at ease, and
tasks that could be done in a flash by anyone else often
got drawn out for hours. Ava's magnetic personality got
even the most unexpected source to become a potential
slow down, from the grocer, to the café waitress, to the
milkman.

The busiest person seemed compelled to let her in on
how their day was going and see what was in store for
hers.

As I approached the ongoing conversation, Ava and
the other two women stopped talking and smiled eagerly.
It prompted me to slow my pace. I nodded reluctantly. I
didn't have the natural warmth Ava did. I gave a little
wave as I approached. "Hi."

The older, more sophisticated of the two women
stepped forward confidently. "Hello, Izzy. We've heard
so much about you. It's nice to finally have the opportunity to meet you in person."

I flushed, wondering what in the world Ava had been
telling these women about me. "Thank you. That's very
kind."

Ava grinned. "Izzy, this is Robin, the visionary behind Twin Oaks' best boutique."

I nodded. "Robin, your shop is so inviting. I can see
why it has been Ava's standing favorite for so long."

Robin looked around proudly. "That's very kind. It's not mine anymore but I like to think I still have an influence."

Ava leaned in closely, as if we weren't the only four people in the store. "I don't think there's a soul in town who doesn't know this place stays on top because of you. The time you were absent was tough for the fashion lovers of this town."

Robin seemed to appreciate Ava's compliment. "Thank you. I feel very fortunate to be back. It gave me purpose and passion after my divorce. I'd be lost without it."

The younger shop girl, who had been listening quietly until now, seemed to be losing her patience. I wasn't sure if she was excited or in need of a restroom, but she began to bounce on the spot, either way.

I turned to face her. "Hi, I'm Izzy."

She smiled at me so broadly I could see her back molars. I reluctantly took a half-step back. She eagerly came forward to close the gap. "Hi, Izzy, I'm Melanie. We've met."

I opened my mouth to speak then closed it silently. In a small community like ours, it was common to run into people we'd met before. But I looked closely at the young woman and nothing came to mind. I blinked then smiled and shook my head. "I'm sorry. I'm drawing a blank."

"It was a few years back and I was just a teenager then."

My forehead rippled with doubt. "Could you refresh

my memory? I don't know how long it's been since I was in that age range. It seems it's catching up with me."

Ava cleared her throat. "It's been fifteen years, Izzy."

I frowned at Ava. "Thank you, old friend. Now Melanie," I said, shifting my attention back to the energetic young woman. "Where did we meet?"

"It was two years ago at the club—Twin Oaks Country Club. You were leaving and stopped to ask me and my friends a few questions about—"

A picture of a younger Melanie in uniform flashed through my mind. I clapped my hands together, inadvertently interrupting her recollection. "I remember. You worked there."

Melanie's eyes lit up. "That's right. You were helping the police with—" She paused and looked around, lowering her voice. "—with the murder investigation."

My nose wrinkled in reaction to her description, well aware the police likely wouldn't have described my actions in quite that manner.

She didn't seem to notice. "You were so cool and confident—I wanted to be like that, too. It wasn't long after that I decided to quit waitressing and enrol at Twin Oaks Community College. I just graduated."

I was flattered. "Good for you. What did you take?"

She raised her chin with pride before she answered. "I couldn't decide so I took family finance to be practical and interior design for fun."

Only then did I notice a pretty ring adorned with a small diamond on her engagement finger. "Ah, it looks like a double congratulations is in order."

Melanie blushed as she held up her hand so I could all take a closer look. "This is the other thing I graduated with."

Ava jumped in. "Melanie's fiancé, Bobby, is working on his accounting designation."

"I never imagined learning about practical money management could lead to love. That's wonderful," I said.

"It sure is," Ava concurred, "However, I must dole out a little advice as an experienced wife of an accountant: spend now. Buy what you don't need before an unromantic and responsible budget is deployed on you."

I grinned. "Sound advice, Ava. Always helping those in no need."

She curtseyed. "We're getting away from our mission here. The point is Melanie has been excited to see you all week and now she has and you feel good."

I looked at Ava suspiciously. "Why didn't you tell me about Melanie? And why didn't you mention this was all set up in advance?"

Ava waved her hand dismissively in the air. "I thought it would be a nice surprise—a fun little reunion. Plus, I thought it would be nice to have things organized for when we got here."

"And now that I'm all buttered up, you think I'll be more inclined to spend money, right?

"No doubt about it."

I looked back to where the change rooms were. "Do you already have outfits picked out that you wanted me to try on?"

She shrugged and nodded affirmatively. "I'm a practical woman—"

I raised my eyebrows.

She continued. "The point is that, as a mother, I have enough in my life to feel guilty about. If my best friend in the world began to share my love of shopping, it would neutralize my moral conscience about the act."

I shook my head. "Sneaky and rather indecent."

She looked at me sideways. "Impressed?"

"Absolutely."

Ava gave me a lopsided grin. "Shall we proceed then?"

I nodded emphatically. "You have succeeded in your quest—I'm feeling good. Let's get shopping."

Robin stepped forward and gently touched my elbow. "Please give us a quick shout if you need anything. Ava is a regular here and knows her way around but we're always here to help. In the meantime, we'll just be in the back sorting through our new order."

I nodded in return. "I appreciate that, thank you. But I'm in good hands. Well, I'm in familiar hands, anyways."

Ava, unfazed by my cheeky comment, saluted the sales ladies and offered me her arm. I happily linked elbows with her and we proceeded to the back of the store, where the clothes hung, awaiting our arrival.

Chapter 3

I looked over the number of dresses already chosen for me to try on in the change area, and I couldn't help but feel excited. I entered one of the small change rooms but before I was able to close the door, Ava came in, too. I looked at her with surprise, uncertain as to why she had joined me in the small room, clearly built for one.

Before I could ask, she took a seat on a small stool, tucked neatly in the corner. She then wiggled her behind on the soft cushion as a mother bird might do when incubating an egg waiting for it to hatch. I watched silently and felt the soft lines between my eyebrows deepen in concern.

"Do I require a chaperone?"

She shook her head back and forth then peeked under the raised door of the small room to make sure we were alone.

"What are you up to?" I demanded.

She suppressed a grin and opened her purse. Tucked

under her wallet was a small parcel. She took it out and unfolded the wrapping. She held up a silky black girdle. "I got you something."

The alarm bells in my mind went off as I looked at the outrageous undergarment. "Have you lost your marbles? I will not put that on. Have some decency, Ava, for goodness sake."

She tried to force it in my hand but I repelled it. "No."

Ava rolled her eyes. "You remind me of my mother sometimes."

I poked at the thing. "Because I have a sense of modesty and respect?"

"Izzy, this little number is going to have you thanking me soon enough. Feel the fabric. It's much lighter and more comfortable than any girdle made before."

I reluctantly reached out and gave it a rub. *Whoa.* I looked up at her. "Okay, it feels nice. It's soft and light. But does it only come in that color?"

"No, but I thought it was a good choice. I got you the matching bra, too. It's almost September, so I knew you wouldn't choose a white dress. I thought it would be kind of fun, don't you think? It's not like anyone else would ever know."

"What I think is that I'm perfectly happy with the ordinary *white* underwear I already have. I mean gee whiz, Ava, black undergarments? Besides, it's too hot out to wear a girdle."

Ava stood up and patted me on the shoulder. "It is today but it won't be in a few weeks. A lot of these dresses are focused on the waistline. A little tug and cinch helps—trust me. Just give it a try. You decide. It can be our little secret."

I reluctantly accepted her gift but insisted on privacy while I changed. Once she left the room, I closed the small door and locked it.

Ava stood on her tiptoes in her high heels and peered over the door. "Hey, I heard that."

I reached up and pinched her nose lightly in irritation. "Then you should know it's meant to keep you out."

She yawned and headed to the nearby coffee maker. It gave me the chance to look over everything in the change room. I quickly ruled out two. A floral number caught my eye and I tried it on. Images of an unmanicured rose bush came to mind, but I came out and did a twirl anyways, determined to maintain a good attitude. Ava shook her head silently and I went back in, feeling relieved. I grabbed the next one—an emerald green cinched-waist dress with a large chiffon underskirt. When I had it on and looked in the mirror, I was relieved to no longer resemble a garden essential yet was still a little underwhelmed. It didn't have quite the shape I hoped it would. I looked sideways at the risqué girdle sitting next to me. I reluctantly grabbed it and put it on under the dress. *Dammit.* Ava was right: it was light, comfortable and, most importantly, gave me the shapely waist I wanted. I silently clapped my hands together. Then, after unsuccessfully trying to contort my shoulders to give me enough reach to do up the long tricky zipper up the back, I gave up and hopped out to show Ava.

She sucked in her breath and grinned. "Gorgeous."

I bit my lip. I couldn't help but agree. I hadn't felt this stylish since my honeymoon. "I think this is it."

"Let's not be hasty, try them all on before deciding. There's no rush."

I decided not to argue. I was having more fun than I expected to, especially since the hard part of choosing what to try had been already done. Before going back in to try on another outfit, our favorite song started playing on the radio. It was a good opportunity to see how the dress would fare on the dance floor. Ava joined me and we had a wordless, impromptu dance-off in the large three-sided mirror situated discreetly within the change area. We took turns showing off our moves as Elvis Presley's "All Shook Up" played on the radio. I imagined this was what it would feel like to be on *American Bandstand.*

Unfortunately, Ava and I were having so much fun we must not have heard the sound of the door chime, used to alert the staff that a customer had entered the shop. My carefree attitude ceased once I heard the newcomer's voice, so distinct in its smugness. I knew instantly who was alerting us to her presence with a hollow laugh. I froze instantly. Ava didn't notice in time and almost toppled over me. I looked up and felt no surprise at the sight of Jane Humphries, the Queen Bee of Twin Oaks Country Club and resident gossip, looking down at us, over the swinging doors, with an expression of superiority. "Don't stop on account of me, ladies."

My cheeks flushed and I tried to smooth my tousled

hair back. "Hi, Jane. Sorry, we didn't hear you."

Her thin arched brows shot up. "Clearly."

Ava stepped forward. She had the enviable trait of not giving a damn what people thought about her—at least not those she disliked. "Jane Humphries. Minding other people's business as usual, I see?"

Standing tall, the polished blonde would certainly be considered attractive, yet her rakish figure and harsh subtleties seemed to block any beauty from coming through the thin veil of disdain. Her beady eyes scrutinized Ava. "Must you have a perpetual bee in your bonnet?"

"Only when I'm near you, honey."

Ava's witty response made me want to giggle but I didn't dare. Since the day I met Jane Humphries, just a few years ago, I was unable to shake an uneasiness that I felt whenever she was in my presence. It brought me right back to my freshman year in high school, when I sometimes just wished I could evaporate on the spot rather than deal with the worry of fitting in with my peers. At least now I had the confidence to somewhat battle the sensation.

I called on it now as Jane turned her attention back to me. "Isabelle, I'm not used to seeing you all dressed up. I assumed you weren't caught up in the silly world of fashion and style. You look rather nice."

Unsure if I was being insulted or complimented, I hesitated in answering.

Ava took the opportunity to step in again. "Izzy could be a real barn burner if she wanted to."

Ava's words propelled me to speak for myself. I

cleared my throat before she could defend me any further. "My birthday is coming up so I thought I might pick up something new."

"How nice. When I reach your age, I will likely be hiding in my bedroom. How very brave of you to celebrate in public."

"Thank you," I peeped with as much gusto as I had left. Evidently, not much remained. I daren't speak up about the fact I was quite certain she was older than me.

The radio seemed to lose its energy, too, and the volume dwindled. A young woman's voice could be heard calling for her mom. It was a relief to see the petition pulled Jane's attention away from us. As she turned on her heel, no discussion was needed for Ava and I to mutually agree the mood had been ruined and we were shopped out. I was confident, however, the green dress I was still wearing could not be beaten. I decided to go ahead and splurge. Ava fully supported the choice.

We made our way up to the front counter quietly in the hopes of not running into the gossip queen again. I kept the chitchat short and sweet, thanking Robin and Melanie for their assistance but ensuring not to linger. Thinking we were scott-free, I was startled when the shop's back room door opened up and Jane reappeared like an unlucky apparition in a dream.

"Ladies, no need to rush off just because of a momentary squabble. My daughter just made a fresh pot of coffee and I've brought some fresh pastries from Betty's on Kerr Street. Why not join us for some morning indulgence?"

Ava and I exchanged looks of confusion. Robin re-garded Melanie, as if looking for an explanation.

Melanie stomped one of her pretty heels on the shop room floor and put her hands on her hips. She faced her mother squarely. "Mom, what do you mean by squabble? What did you do?"

Jane eased forward gently and began to stroke Mela-nie's hair dotingly; in a way I would've thought her inca-pable of. "Darling, I just hadn't realized anyone was in the change-room. I caught the ladies off-guard. There was nothing sinister in my actions, promise."

Melanie swiped her mother's hand away like she might a pestering fly. "We've talked about this, Mother." The young associate then turned back to face Ava and me. "My mom seems unable to leave our customers alone. She means no harm by intruding on your shopping time. And I'm certain it won't happen again."

Jane conceded and failed in an attempt at, what I guessed was, a congenial smile in our direction. "Melanie is right. As she mentioned, I like to greet her customers. You ladies know I'm a very friendly person."

Melanie folded her arms over her chest.

Jane stammered. "T—The point is I apologize for barging in on you, Isabelle and Ava."

I automatically looked at Ava. Her face had changed from sullen to bright. Apparently watching her least fa-vorite person in town squirm was a mood lifter. I caught a glimpse of my own grinning face in a nearby mirror. Yup, it seemed to have worked for me, too.

I allowed my smile to steer toward Jane. I could see

she was anxiously awaiting us to let her off the hook. I let her twist in the wind, just for a minute. "That is kind of you, Jane."

Ava stepped forward. "And so humble."

Jane pressed her lips together. "Yes, Melanie is encouraging me to be a little more relaxed."

Melanie patted her mom's hand. "Mom is trying to show Robin that she can be friendly and not overbearing so she's allowed to visit me at the store."

"An exercise I wouldn't need to do if you spent more time at home, dear. I barely get to see you anymore," Jane said.

As much as I was entertained by observing Jane humbled by her daughter, my instinct to avoid her was stronger. "You three enjoy your morning break. Ava and I are due at the club to meet a few friends."

Jane was visibly relieved. Her expression seemed to prompt Ava to respond. "Izzy, I think we can spare enough time for a treat."

I locked arms with her. "Nope, we can't."

She frowned at me. I began to pull her away. Robin grabbed a small datebook and a pencil. "Izzy, when would you like to come back so we can tailor your dress?"

I paused. "Is there much to do?"

Robin shook her head. "I doubt it. I'm a pretty efficient alteration hand. A few nips and tucks will give it the perfect fit."

"Is tomorrow morning too soon?" I asked.

Robin jotted it in her book. "No, it's perfect. I'll see you then."

We bid the ladies good-bye, and I dragged Ava from the shop, well aware she was disappointed that we didn't stay to watch Jane squirm. "You know it's quite unlike you to bask in pleasure at the sight of a woman's discomfort."

She rolled her eyes. "Jane is the most judgemental, entitled person I've ever encountered. There are few people I truly dislike. She happens to be one of them. So I won't apologize for wanting to be present on the rare occasion she doesn't feel ten feet above anyone else in the room."

I couldn't argue. She was right. "Seeing as we are done shopping already, shall we validate our story?"

She paused tying her scarf and looked at me. "Sometimes it scares me how much we think alike. To the club?"

I revved the engine, put the car in first gear, and took off. "You got it."

Chapter 4

We didn't need to call ahead to find out if our dear friend, Mary Whitmore, would be at the Twin Oaks Country Club for lunch. It was part of her daily routine. She was a little older and a lot wealthier than either one of us but neither her age nor her circumstances ever got in the way of the tight-knit friendship we had developed during the war. Working and living together at a munitions factory cemented a friendship over a decade earlier. Our loyalty and affections for one another remained as strong as ever.

We arrived at the town's private club a few minutes later. After years of avoiding social invitations by Mary to join her, Ava and I finally acquiesced. The experience was surprisingly fun and enjoyable—not stuffy and formal as I had expected.

Mary's youthful energy and light spirit were easy to spot. She was sitting with a few ladies, evidently having coffee or tea, looking bright and cheery. Her short, blond, curly locks and tailored silk white blouse complemented her beautiful complexion, especially paired with the red and blue scarf she had tied stylishly around her neck. Her hazel eyes almost seemed to dance in delight as she caught a glimpse of us from across the room. She excused herself and came to greet us.

"My two favorite troublemakers. What a wonderful surprise. It's not Tuesday, is it?" Mary asked giving each of a quick welcoming embrace. We met here weekly for lunch—a habit we started about a year earlier along with the fourth in our foursome, Jo Reynolds, a girl Friday and occasional columnist over at the local newspaper.

Ava pointed at me. "No, but we completed our day's mission early and decided it was the perfect opportunity to come by and invite ourselves to your morning retreat."

Mary's head tilted to the side. "I'm so glad you did. Now you must come and sit down to divulge this mission of yours."

She led us to an empty table that had sliding glass doors nearby, opening up to a lovely garden, then skillfully garnered the attention of a passing server and ordered some light sandwiches and coffee all around. "Now, please satisfy my curiosity by telling me what you two were up to this morning."

"Ava might have set you up just to let you down. It was just shopping," I said.

Mary looked suspicious. "That all depends. Where were you shopping and what did you buy?"

Ava leaned forward. "Izzy finally came with me to Robin's Closet. She got herself a lovely outfit for tomorrow night."

Mary tapped my hand as if scolding a child. "And you said it was just shopping. Ava, you have much to teach our young apprentice."

Ava let out a puff of air. "I appreciate your support."

I spotted a familiar figure not far away and was happy to have a reason to shift the attention away from me. "Girls, there's Barbara Wiggins. The actual owner of the store I seem to lack an appreciation of."

Ava shook her head. "I'm not surprised. She was never one to choose work over fun."

Mary cleared her throat. We knew that meant there was more to it. We sat back and waited to be filled in.

She looked around to make sure we were out of earshot of anyone else. "Apparently, Barbara's husband, Walter, started complaining about how much time she was spending at the store. He told some of his golf buddies that he regretted allowing her to buy it—thought it would just be a fun little hobby for her. But she regularly started getting home late and wouldn't have dinner made before eight. I guess he was bored and began coming here after work, indulging himself at the bar. By the time he got home, he was often inebriated. Naturally, that led to quarrels between the couple. She would call him a drunk, and he would complain about everything from a lack of attention to her aging figure. According to a few of the ladies, Barbara said Walter was behaving like such a creep, she was going to teach him a lesson. No details were divulged, but that was right around the time she stopped spending her days at the store, and started coming here instead—that was six or eight months ago."

My curiosity was piqued. If what Mary heard was true, I expected there could be a big pushback from Mrs. Wiggins. In our earlier days, Barbara didn't take kindly to anyone who challenged her, and I doubted it would be any different now.

Ava must have read my mind. "Mr. Wiggins better watch out. There's a storm on the horizon."

Mary looked concerned. "I suppose you would know—you two were quite close when you were younger, weren't you?"

Ava clicked her tongue. "Oh, the tales I could tell."

I nodded in agreement; my eyes wide with emphasis.

Mary smiled. "Girls, you're being a bit dramatic, aren't you? Perhaps Barbara has matured and rearranged her priorities. She was probably just blowing off a little steam with the ladies. Besides, that was almost a year ago. Nothing ever came of it."

Ava and I exchanged a look. We simultaneously shook our heads, agreeing to disagree with Mary. I didn't know Barbara as well as Ava, but I knew enough to doubt Mary's logical deduction.

Mary looked amused at our reaction. "I guess only time will tell."

I wondered if Barbara's husband had any idea what might be coming his way."

Chapter 5

The next morning, I was tidying up the kitchen thinking about the night's upcoming dinner with the girls.

As I waited for my tea to steep, I heard shuffling at the front door. I heard it open slowly and stretched my neck out just in time to see Ava scour the room silently.

"Olly Olly Oxen Free…" she whispered.

My eyes followed her and I wondered if there was something I was missing. "Ava?"

I called out. "I hope you aren't expecting me to know what you're up to, because I haven't the faintest clue."

Her eyebrows shot up and she shushed me as she crept forward into the kitchen. "Geez, Izzy. For someone who has had a hand at solving a crime or two, you can be really obtuse. I'm asking if the damned coast is clear."

"Clear from who?"

"The kids, of course. I want to make sure neither one is home unexpectedly. I don't want them to think I'm trying to corrupt their mother."

"My kids are well aware you stole my natural sensibilities long before they were born."

She stood tall. "Say it ain't so."

"Oh, please. Katherine was rolling her eyes at us by the time she was twelve. At fifteen, she dismissed the idea you or I even attended finishing school."

Ava frowned. "At what point did she begin to suspect me in your moral failings?"

"Probably the day she caught you topping off your tea with whiskey? How old was she then, seven?"

Ava stammered. "I—I had a cough. Everyone knows a hot toddy kills colds." She eyed my tea and feigned a cough. "Speaking of..."

I raised my hands. "I've got places to be. But I'm glad you're here. Now you can join me."

She pulled a gift from behind her back and passed it over. "Not before you open your present."

I clapped my hands and followed her instructions. Underneath a brightly wrapped box, complete with a big red ribbon, was the most beautiful pair of high-heeled shoes I had ever set my eyes on. They were a shimmery gold color and taller than any I had previously worn. I couldn't wait to get these stick-heeled shoes on my feet. I looked at Ava with a wide smile. "You devil."

"See why I was trying to avoid the kids?"

I wasn't able to look at Ava while she spoke. I was far too distracted putting my new shoes on. "I most certainly do. Of course, you know they adore you, bad influence or not."

She smiled. "They'd better. They're the only kids

I've ever loved—other than my own angels, of course."

I stood up and walked shakily over to the full-length mirror inside the closet, next to the front door.

She came over to take a look and steadied my wobble at the same time. "Why don't you practice walking in the house a little bit before dinner?"

She was right. This may take some getting used to. "How come Cinderella didn't tip over? She couldn't have been used to shoes like this."

"Hold on a second. If you're the young princess, that makes me the much older, fairy Godmother. I object. Besides, I'd never give you a midnight curfew. One a.m. is much more reasonable."

"Oh shoot! That reminds me—what time is it?"

Ava leaned over the sofa and craned her neck to read the kitchen clock. "It's almost eleven. Lots of time to stabilize."

"No, no, I have to go. I have my alteration appointment at Robin's Closet. Do you want to come?"

"Do you need to ask?"

I swapped out the sparklers for my sensible ballet flats. "Okay, c'mon, I'll drive. You're too slow—maybe it's the elderly godmother in you."

Ava gave me a warning look. "Cut that out."

I grinned and fluttered my eyelashes innocently. "Oh, dear, are you getting sensitive in your old age?"

"Dammit, never show weakness to the enemy. I forgot. Fine, just let this granny apply some lipstick before you give me whiplash. I want to look good for the ambulance crew."

She puckered, I grabbed my new shoes, and together we rushed out the door.

Chapter 6

We got to Robin's Closet fast just in time for my appointment. The store should've been open at least an hour, but it was evident upon our arrival that that was certainly not the case. Although the door was slightly ajar, the lights were not yet on, the radio wasn't playing, and the fans hadn't begun to circulate the rather stifling air. Ava and I looked at each other, hesitant as to whether we should even step inside. Ava took a peek and walked in. I followed behind.

We looked around and I stepped forward. "Hello?"

Barbara Wiggins popped her head out from the back. There was a scowl on her face. "Nice to have you finally grace us with your presence. You better have a damn good reason for arriving late this morning. I will not—" She stopped mid-sentence as soon as she saw it was us and not the employee she was obviously expecting. Her scowl faded and was replaced with a smile. "Oh dear, I'm so sorry, ladies. Give me one second back here."

Barbara's face disappeared briefly before she

emerged from the back of the shop, wearing a rather out-of-place looking tennis dress. She smoothed her ash blonde bobbed hair and gave us each a small hug. "Apologies, girls. I thought you were my tardy shop girl."

Ava looked amused. "The outrage you must feel at having to work at your own business. Did you actually have to interrupt a game to be here?"

Having known Barbara Wiggins most of her life, Ava obviously felt comfortable speaking her mind. Of course, it was rare that she didn't.

Barbara took a half step back as she looked at Ava with her mouth slightly ajar. I held my breath. Ava's chin protruded and she met Barbara's gaze with raised eyebrows. They locked eyes for a moment, then a grin broke out on Barbara's face as she shook her head and relaxed her shoulders. "You're lucky we were sorority sisters, Ava. Why, I'm sure you're aware I am not accustomed to being spoken to like that."

Ava couldn't help but mimic Barbara's grin. "Well, someone has to remind you to smile, don't they?"

Barbara conceded. "I suppose, but I'm frustrated, Ava. I let Robin run my shop as if it were still hers. But if she's going to take advantage of that, I'll fire her without a second thought. After all, she is as replaceable as the next sales girl. Sometimes, I think she forgets that."

Barbara's attitude toward the woman who ran her business struck me as harsh and unkind. It was a reminder of why I had never been especially fond of her.

My sentiments didn't seem to be shared. Ava had let it slide and moved onto her admiration of Barbara's outfit. "Izzy, do you see this? I never considered tennis before but perhaps this unexpected meeting is fate's way of guiding me to lasting physical fitness."

"Serendipitous," I noted dryly.

"Sarah who?" she asked, clearly distracted as she examined the pleats on Barbara's skirt.

I shook my head as the ladies discussed tennis fashion. I wandered over to the front window and looked outside. My attention was drawn to a woman who was sitting on a bench, covering her face with her hands pressed so firmly above her forehead that the tips of her fingers were white. I almost fell over when the subject of my interest looked up and met my gaze. It was Robin Manners. She looked downright panicked now that I had seen her. I put my finger on my lips and excused myself from the store. I approached and saw her tears had stopped but she was left with just blotchy skin and a shaky demeanor. My heart went out to her.

She looked behind me, to see if anyone else was coming from the store. I guessed she knew she would be in for an unpleasant greeting when she arrived. "Is Barbara in there fuming?"

"Yes, but don't worry about that right now. Are you okay?" I asked.

Her shaky hand tried to push away the notion. "I'm fine, really, Izzy. It's just sometimes, at the most mundane moments, it strikes me that I'm alone. It's been two years since my divorce. How much longer will I feel like this? What's worse is my embarrassment—I'm sorry to be insensitive to your loss. I can't imagine how difficult it must've been when you lost your husband."

I rubbed her arm, trying to soothe her frazzled state. Very aware of the emotion she was experiencing. "It's been four years for me and I'm just getting on my feet now. But our situations are not dissimilar. We both experienced the loss of our life partner—just in different ways. You have challenges I can't imagine. I know how unkind people can be at times."

She studied my face. "Or how kind. Thank you."

I rubbed her shoulder and she held an extended blink and let all the breath exit her body. Her jaw locked. Then she hung her head. "I can't have children. I'm barren."

My hand cupped my mouth.

She continued to look at the ground. "The doctors couldn't tell me why, and I couldn't stay married to a man who wanted so desperately to be a father."

My heart broke for her. "I'm so sorry."

She pulled her head up to look at me. "Thank you. I've made my peace with it now. I'm lucky enough to have maintained a good friendship with my ex-husband. It was my decision. He would've stuck by me but I couldn't live with myself. It didn't feel right. Anyways, he was more than generous with me—left me with more money than I could ever hope for, in fact. But it's hard. He's remarried now and he just called to divulge that his new wife is pregnant.

"He didn't want me to hear it from someone else. Certain gestures like that one makes me doubt he'll ever love his wife the way he loved me, but that could be something I just tell myself now to get through moments like this."

I didn't know what to say so I stayed quiet and allowed her to release what she needed to.

Through fresh tears she smiled at me. "Anyways, I knew this day was coming. I have since found fulfillment through other passions," she said, indicating the shop.

I nodded supportively. "Robin, it comes through. That's why everyone in town loves the store. You found your calling. You make people feel their best—feel special. Not everyone can do that."

She tapped my knee. "Thank you for listening, Izzy."

"You're welcome."

A lukewarm smile spread across her face. "I think it's time I face the music." She stood up. "Then we can move on to your dress. It will look stunning when I'm done. Just a few nips and tucks is all it will take."

I was impressed with her ability to regain composure so quickly. I was also relieved. I just hoped Robin could withstand the wrath of Barbara Wiggins. I supposed after the heartache she'd experienced already, a few snarky comments from Barbara might slide off her back like melted butter.

As we approached the entranceway, I peered into the same window that I had first spotted Robin. Barbara and Ava were still chatting happily but I noticed Ava now subtly looking over toward us. She caught my eye as we approached and gave me the slightest nod that only two best friends might detect. I knew it was her way of telling me things were okay. I felt a huge wave of relief. When

Robin and I entered there were no harsh words or reprimands. Barbara was too busy laughing it up with her old sorority sister. When Robin offered a sincere apology, Barbara was in such good spirits she dismissed her lateness as no big deal, stating everyone makes mistakes from time to time.

Ava later told me she had to re-enact her own misguided attempts at crooning during a talent show at a prestigious summer camp to loosen Barbara up and remind her not to take things oh-so-seriously. Although Ava refused to do a repeat performance for me, I silently thanked goodness for being awarded such a kind-spirited best friend.

Robin wasted no time getting organized to make the adjustments on my dress. She had her tomato pincushion out and, within seconds, I was standing on a small wooden box in front of a mirror, holding my arms out like a scarecrow. I watched as she pondered a few angles. She began to pin the dress, and it looked so close to my stomach I couldn't refrain from trying to dodge the anticipated pinch. I felt like an animated voodoo doll. Ava giggled and Robin patiently told me to stop moving. She reminded me of a wizard, working her magic with a needle instead of a wand. When she was done, my waist looked cinched and the dress looked perfect—I was surprised at what a dramatic difference it made. Needless to say, I was thoroughly pleased. Robin carefully took the dress off me and went to the back of the shop, where she would make the alterations more permanent.

Chapter 7

With the promise of just a few minutes to finish the alterations to my dress, Ava found a few items she couldn't resist trying on. I watched her, happy to have a break from the full-length mirror and mannequin duties. I was helping her out of a particularly snug fitting number when the bells on the shop door jingled.

"Barbara!" a man shouted angrily.

Ava and I looked at each other with concern.

"Barbara, get out here right now!" he shouted without giving pause to wait for a response from his initial outburst.

It was jarring. Ava changed quickly and we quietly made our way to the swinging doors of the change area. We peeked over the top. Barbara hadn't yet shown her face. I couldn't blame her. Walter Wiggins, Barbara's tall heavy-set, balding husband, was standing in the middle of the shop, clutching his fedora in one hand and shaking his fist with the other. His face was bright red and his angry expression was unapologetic and bold. His eyes darted around the room. I ducked down quickly behind the swinging doors. Ava's tall figure wasn't as quick to drop.

I heard heavy footsteps walk toward us.

"Barbara, is that you? Don't play games with me. I'm in no mood."

Ava and I simultaneously pushed open the swinging doors and came face-to-face with Walter.

He pressed his lips together, lowered his eyebrows and dropped his chin. He was seething. "Where is my wife?"

Before we could say anything, Barbara stepped out from the back room. She didn't look as flustered as I felt. In fact, it didn't look like she was anything but amused. "For heaven's sake, Walter, settle down. I'm right here."

He stammered and faced his wife, obviously miffed she wasn't intimidated by his demanding presence. He tried to stand even taller, reminding me of a gorilla ready to beat his chest, seemingly trying to demand a threatening presence yet unable to gain the upper hand. When it didn't work, he took a step back and pointed at her menacingly. "Barbara, we need to talk in private—now."

She fluttered her eyelashes and smiled coyly. "Should I steep some tea?"

"Dammit woman, don't play games with me."

Barbara looked downright bored. "Yes, dear." She looked at Ava and me. "Ladies, could I trouble you to borrow the change area for a few minutes? Robin is working in the back and my husband seems to be a little short of both time and manners."

We nodded in assent and stepped aside. Barbara held her head high and led the way. Walter trailed behind, his nostrils flaring.

Robin slipped out from the back and silently joined Ava and me. Her pale face and puzzled expression told me this wasn't a regular occurrence. The three of us watched with bated breath.

"Well, you've made your presence known, Walter. Do you want to tell me what your unexpected visit is all about?" Barbara demanded.

"Why has the rent for this place not been paid in four months?"

"Has it not?"

"Don't play dumb. I demand to know."

"It must've slipped my mind. Being a woman, there's a limit to my abilities. Isn't that what you told me?"

"Barbara," he said in a warning tone.

She didn't seem to notice. "Perhaps it's my age. I'm no spring chicken, Walter. You've said so yourself."

He paused. "It's not just the rent. Bob Cole down at the bank told me the angry suppliers are starting to call him, too."

"Well, that can't be a good thing."

"No, Barb, it's not a good thing. Bob says the bills are adding up and has asked me to step in and sort it out. Apparently, he has tried to get in touch with you but you haven't been calling him back."

"Oh, dear, he's right. I assumed he was calling to make dinner plans at the club. I was trying to put it off.

You know I find his wife Lucy a bit of a bore—"

There was a loud cracking sound as Walter punched the wall. I jumped.

"Barbara!" Walter yelled with a shaky voice, "Get down to the bank and sort this out—now! You've got one hour."

With that, he bulldozed his way through the change area swinging doors, almost knocking them off their hinges. He walked out the front door without so much as a glance around. I guessed all he could see was red.

Barbara quietly followed a minute later, a smug look of satisfaction spread across her face. "Apologies, ladies. My husband is a little upset."

I stepped forward. "Are you okay, Barbara?"

She looked at me and took a deep breath. "Izzy, I feel better right now than I have in years."

Robin approached Barbara after Walter left so abruptly. She gently touched her arm, "I'm sure you'll sort it out."

Barbara pulled her arm away slowly. "I'm not going to the bank, if that's what you are suggesting. I have to be on the court in thirty minutes. Because of you, I've lost one game already. I'm not planning on missing another."

Robin looked confused.

Barbara smiled at her. "If you are so worried about what Walter said, why don't *you* go down to the bank?"

Robin looked confused. "But Walter said—"

Barbara looked sharply at Robin. "Walter says lots of things. But he's not your boss—I am."

Robin nodded. "Okay, Barbara. I'm sure there's nothing to worry about, anyways. We're busier than ever. It must be some sort of accounting glitch at the bank."

A hint of smile crept up on Barbara's face. "Wouldn't it be embarrassing for my husband if it weren't—downright humiliating, really."

Robin looked in utter disbelief from Barbara to me. Did we just witness Barbara getting back at her husband? It would certainly prove Barbara would pull no punches when she was determined to win. The disturbing thought haunted me for the rest of the afternoon.

Chapter 8

In spite of the stressful day, I was in a great mood by nightfall. After a long bath, I was feeling relaxed and flicked on the radio. I took my time getting ready for the evening ahead and set the mood with some music. Never one for a soft melody, I momentarily wondered if the loud volume would cause a raised eyebrow from my neighbors. Dismissing the thought, I had a one-man dance party as Ricky Nelson and Elvis serenaded me with their catchy tunes. When it was time to go, I soaked up the light perspiration and flushed cheeks with my trusted Pan-Cake make-up and thanked Max Factor for allowing me to keep my face respectable while having a little fun.

I arrived at The Mariner's Whisper at six. It was the best dinner club in town. I could feel the energy wafting through the door as I approached, with upbeat jazz music setting the tone, and Clifford Brown's trumpet adding a little sass to my step. I peered over the crowd waiting to be seated and saw that Ava, Mary, and Jo were already here. I didn't wait for an escort, making my way to our regular table, available to us whenever we dined there, as long as we gave a little notice.

When the head chef was murdered a few years earlier, the four of us helped the police solve the case. The standing reservation was a way to say thank you. It was the best seat in the house, located on the raised level that gave a panoramic overview of the whole restaurant. Needless to say, it inspired us to come back regularly. Since it was my birthday, we had agreed to make a night of it. I could see as I approached that the tone had already been set with dimmed candles sitting in the middle of the table, and lovely smiles all around. I grinned in anticipation of the night ahead and opened my arms to virtually embrace my three best friends, each looking her best.

Before I was close enough to voice a hello, an unexpected sound grabbed my attention from a nearby table. It was a gasp. I wouldn't have paused my intended path had the woman who uttered the sound not displayed such an expression of terror on her face. I turned to see where her attention was focused. A jolt shot up my body and my hands shot up to cover my mouth. All thoughts of my birthday were abandoned as I rushed back to help Walter Wiggins, who had just stumbled into the restaurant, screaming for help. By the time I reached him, the band had stopped playing. His loud cries were the only sound now detectable as people instinctively backed away silently, the lifeless body of Barbara draped across his arms, covered in blood.

Walter was shaking from head-to-toe. A sense of determined calm kicked in as I locked eyes with him momentarily and I recognized his raw fear and panic. I leaned in and gently cradled my hand under Barbara's neck. Her eyes were closed but there was what looked to be a welt near the back of her head that was slowly seeping blood. He had stopped screaming upon my approach but his eyes continued to dart around unfocused.

I tried to guide his attention by pressing on his shoulder firmly. "Walter, Walter, do you remember me? I'm Isabelle Walsh. I need you to gently and carefully lie Barbara down."

Although he failed to respond verbally, he did his best to follow my instructions. He bent down on one knee and laid her across the floor. I crouched down on the other side and swept matted hair off her face. I looked up and saw the restaurant owner, Harriet Smith, standing nearby. I was relieved to see her pale yet calm face. Her attention was focused on me. "Harriet, I need you to see if there is a doctor here."

She turned around and called out for a doctor or a medic. A man near the back of the restaurant stood up, raising his hand. She requested his presence, and he made his way over, obviously unaware of what had happened until he was almost on top of us. As he did so, Harriet instructed a nearby waiter to call the police.

The doctor told everyone to back up and give him space. I gently pulled Walter to his feet as the doctor knelt down so he could examine his unexpected patient without interference. A basic check of her vitals and a subtle look at her head wound told him what he had been summoned to find out. He looked up at me, his lips pressed tightly together, and shook his head back and forth. He confirmed what I already knew. Barbara Wiggins was dead.

Walter's eyes filled with tears. He grabbed on to me—wailing so frantically, I almost fell over. Luckily, I felt a firm hand come from behind just in time. I turned my head to see Ava holding me up, with Jo and Mary on either side of her. It gave me the courage and strength I needed right then to support this terrified man whose life had just been torn apart.

Chapter 9

A short time later, the ambulance came and took Barbara's lifeless body from the restaurant. Walter wanted to escort his departed wife's body, but the police, who had also arrived, would not allow it. The newly widowed man was so shaken up, I stayed next to him in case I could offer any assistance. He must've taken some comfort in my presence, since when I excused myself to briefly splash some water on my face, he looked panicked and asked me to come back quickly. I guessed since I was the first one to respond to his call for help, he felt some assurance from my presence among the chaos and noise of the unfolding scene.

I hadn't had the opportunity to actually speak to my friends yet since the commotion started, so when I spotted them as I exited the restroom, I scooted over to check in. Before I had a chance to say anything, Walter, who had been scanning the restaurant, caught my eye. His eyebrows raised hopefully, and I tried to mollify him by holding up my index finger to indicate I'd be over shortly. He looked disappointed but attempted a frail smile.

Ava grabbed my elbow abruptly and pulled me into the booth where she, Mary, and Jo were sitting, just out of reach from the ongoing chaos. "Are you all right? What the heck happened? We can't seem to get a straight answer from anyone."

"I'm fine but unfortunately Barbara is not," I answered distractedly as I looked over at Walter whose laser eyes had caught sight of me again.

Mary cupped her hand over mine. "Izzy, what exactly do you mean?"

I looked at her apologetically as I stood up, seconds after sitting down. "Barbara is dead. I'm trying to find out what happened, but as of yet, I don't know. I hate to leave it there but I've got to get back to Walter. Can I meet you guys after at Mary's if we get separated?"

Mary nodded vehemently. "Yes, of course."

Jo stood up and cleared her throat. "The police are systematically clearing the restaurant. We tucked ourselves back here to stall our exit so we could talk to you. Now that we have, we'll go. But don't forget to take care of yourself. You're under no obligation to remain here once the police clear you to leave."

"I'm fine, Jo," I lied.

Her chin dropped as her eyebrows raised. "Izzy, you're shaking like a leaf. It's not just your face that gives you away."

I hugged her tiny, almost boy-like frame and nodded. Then I took a deep breath and walked back to Walter.

He was standing beside a familiar face—Detective

Henry Jones. The detective looked up to see who had taken Walter's attention away. He blinked twice, which for him was like someone else dropping their jaw open. "Mrs. Walsh?"

I could understand why Detective Jones looked puzzled. It wasn't our first meeting at the scene of a murder. The perpetually rugged, unshaven detective scanned me with his dark eyes. I felt a flush rise in my cheeks as I demanded that my eyes meet his. I held my breath, just for a second.

"Hi, Detective Jones."

There were no further words exchanged between us. I stood on the other side of Walter, who looked relieved at my return. I gave the broken man a reassuring nod. I hoped it would give him just enough support to get through the day, at least until a better advocate for him could be found.

He looked back at the detective. "Mrs. Walsh came to my aid when everyone else backed away. I'd like her nearby."

The detective nodded, without looking at me. "Of course, Mr. Wiggins. Now, we need to get back to our talk. You said that you and Mrs. Wiggins were walking along the pier?"

"Yes, we were on our way here, in fact."

"How did your wife get hurt?"

"We were just walking and something dropped from above us—from the Cooper's Bridge. It came out of nowhere and hit Barbara on the head."

The detective nodded. "What was the object that hit her?"

Mr. Wiggins threw his hands up, clearly distraught. "I don't know. It happened so quickly."

Detective Jones reached out and calmly but firmly gripped the man's elbow lowering it back down. The other arm followed suit. "I need you to close your eyes, sir, and try to visualize the object in your mind."

"Okay." Mr. Wiggins complied. "We were walking and talking when it hit my wife. She was like a rag doll, the way it knocked her down. She never saw it coming. I fell to my knees beside her and saw the blood on her head. That's when I looked over to see what hit her…"

"Go on, Mr. Wiggins," Detective Jones said quietly.

Walter closed his eyes. "Yes, I see it now. It was a metal bar. It was shaped like a 'T.' The smaller side was rounded and had spikes on the sides like some type of medieval weapon."

The detective wrote down the description. I drew the shape in the palm of my left hand with my right index finger. Then I turned my hand upside down. Instantly, I recognized a familiar shape. "Mr. Wiggins, could the object that hit Barbara be an anchor?"

He opened his eyes and met mine. "Yes, of course. Why didn't I recognize that? We had just been on our sailboat, for God's sake."

Detective Jones looked from me to Walter. "Sometimes in a moment of crisis, the brain can only absorb so much information. It can take time for details to process. It makes sense that you might not immediately recognize a familiar object, especially if it's in an unexpected place."

Mr. Wiggins looked at the detective angrily. "Why would someone throw an anchor over the bridge so carelessly?"

The detective shook his head. "That's a question I can't answer yet, I'm afraid."

I had an idea. "Detective Jones, wouldn't it be smart to go there now—see if the anchor is still there?"

Mr. Wiggins eyes began to dart around. "Dear God, you're right. It might even have Barbara's blood on it. Sir, please, allow me to go there—show you where my beautiful wife was struck down."

Detective Jones gave me a warning look before facing Mr. Wiggins. "That was next on my list—if you're up to it."

Mr. Wiggins stamped his feet. "I'm not up to any of this. But if it will help find the idiot who, so carelessly, took my wife from me, I'm willing to do whatever it takes."

Detective Jones put his notebook away. "Okay. Give me a minute to organize things here. Mrs. Walsh, might I have a word?"

I nodded and followed him out of earshot of Walter.

He cleared his throat. "I'd like you to accompany Mr. Wiggins on our little walk. He seems to have latched onto you as a source of comfort, and I need you to keep him as calm and focused as possible. Every detail and every minute counts right now. Can we count on you?"

I looked him in the eye and nodded. "Yes, Detective Jones. I'll do my best."

"Good. And keep your eyes and ears open. If you see anything that strikes you as relevant, remember it. I'll need you to come down to the station afterward and give a statement."

"Is there anything in particular I should be looking for, aside from the obvious?" I asked.

"Just stay alert. And, if you see anyone—anyone at all, stay away and let me know immediately."

His words gave me chills. "Got it."

"One more thing—leave the itinerary to me from now on, capiche?"

I bit my lip and nodded. We walked back to Walter. The detective slapped him on the back assertively. "Okay, Mr. Wiggins, let's go."

The detective turned and gave instructions to make sure no one entered the restaurant or went near where Barbara's body had been. He then indicated for two officers to accompany us. We were out the door in seconds. On the walk over, the detective took the opportunity to ask Walter a few more questions. "Could you tell me if there was a particular reason you chose this location to walk tonight? Was it planned in advance?"

"It was our weekly routine," Walter answered. "We always sat on our boat, had some wine, and then went to the restaurant. We had a standing reservation—although tonight was a little different. Barbara and I were celebrating with champagne instead of our usual red wine."

"What were you celebrating?"

Walter swallowed hard and scrunched his eyes together as if protecting his eyes in a windstorm. He managed to keep the tears back. "We were celebrating our marriage. You see, we'd had an ongoing disagreement and finally found the perfect solution. We had been to the bank to settle some affairs then on to our sailboat docked along the shore. We had some champagne and were going to continue the celebration with dinner—we even talked about taking a spin on the dance floor. We hadn't done that in probably ten years."

Detective Jones studied Mr. Wiggins face. It was impossible to guess what the experienced officer was thinking, but I could see his focus was razor sharp. "Mind telling me how you came to a resolution?"

"Not at all. I closed her business."

"And that was a mutual decision?" Detective Jones asked.

"No," Walter admitted. "But once it was tempered with the promise of a trip to Monte Carlo, she came around."

The detective nodded. "Sounds like an expensive compromise."

"Not compared to what her business venture cost me."

I looked at the detective. "But the store was so popular."

Walter cleared his throat. "I'm afraid my wife hadn't paid the bills in some time, in spite of the profits coming in. She had decided to spend the money that was meant to pay the bills on other things. It was her way of showing me she was angry for some mistakes I had made. After calculating the cost of defaulting payments and my personal reputation with the bank, a trip overseas was an easy decision—much better than the risk of another future lesson from my beloved."

The detective took a few notes but didn't ask any more questions. Within a few minutes, the sun had set and a dark silence enveloped us as we approached the path near the bridge.

Mr. Wiggins began to visibly shake and slow his gait as we evidently reached the scene of the accident. It looked like he was using all his strength to stay focused and present, probably wishing he could crawl into a hole somewhere and pretend this was just a bad dream. He stopped walking. "It happened here, where I now stand."

The detective looked at him. "Okay."

I looked around the well-lit path and saw a dark object lying on the ground, just out of the spotlight, not three feet away. My arm stretched out as my index finger began to point. "Is that…"

The detective moved toward the object as the widower backed away. Sure enough, there was an old-looking anchor sitting at the edge of the path, where the grass led up to the bridge. It was large enough to see how the heavy metal object could cause a fatal injury, especially if dropped from the bridge above the walkway, thirty feet above.

Detective Jones ordered everyone to stand back. He crouched down to examine the anchor. In the dark it was hard to see from where we stood. The only area properly lit was the walkway along the pier. The detective then looked up at the bridge and back down to where the anchor lay, as if trying to work out how such a tragedy could have taken place.

A few sailboats were docked along the pier. I noticed one not far from where we stood had decorative lighting on it, illuminating the name of the vessel, *High Society*, and a small table set up for two on the deck.

"Walter, is that your boat? The one you and Barbara were on earlier?" I asked.

He nodded then turned away. We stood quietly as the thick sea air slowly enveloped us.

Within a few minutes, the detective instructed the accompanying officers to bring Walter and me back to the restaurant. We did as we were told. I looked back, just for a moment, and saw Detective Jones carefully pick up the anchor with his gloved hand and walk onto the grass and up the steep hill where the bridge began. Now too dark to see, he disappeared into the night, and I turned back toward the lights, holding the arm of the quiet, broken man.

The walk back to the restaurant was filled with undisturbed silence. I guessed poor Walter was done talking for the night. After what was, no doubt, the worst night of his life, I hoped the police would let him soon go home and take solace in his grief. When Detective Jones returned, a few minutes later, he did just that. Before I said good-bye, I asked if Walter if he wanted me to contact a friend or family member for him. He dismissed the offer, desiring privacy to grieve alone. He thanked me for my help and left. I didn't linger either, glad to take my leave and head out.

It was not even nine o'clock when I got home but it felt much later. I was desperate to get my heels off and peel out of my dress. I called Mary and postponed meeting up until the morning. Then I changed into my favorite flannel nightgown and lit a fire. Tired or not, there were details of the night I wanted to get down on paper so they didn't slip my mind. I curled up on the soft, cozy sofa with a pen and paper, and began to go write down each and every moment I could remember of the night. I wasn't sure why, but I felt it may be important in the days to come.

I opened my eyes, wondering at what point they had closed. I looked down at the paper. There was the beginning of a singular word and then just a pen mark—a line leading down to the bottom of the page where my hand must've fallen off as I fell asleep. I looked at my watch. Two-thirty am. So much for that idea. I was chilly and noticed the fire had gone out. I knew when to recognize defeat. I dragged myself off the sofa and to my bed where I didn't even have the chance to formulate a plan for the morning.

What felt like seconds later I awoke to a loud barrage of knocking coming from my front door. I was desperately trying to change out of my nightgown when I heard Ava call my name. Relief set in and I abandoned my efforts to appear decent. I opened the door to Ava, Mary, and Jo all fully dressed and accompanied by one of my favorite things in the world—coffee. I felt my shoulders relax and give them a very welcoming smile. I ushered in the fresh cup of java and my best friends, to boot.

It was a comforting start to the day after such a tragic night.

Before I could even take a sip, Ava took my warm cup and placed it down on the nearby tray. She then embraced me like we were long lost sisters.

It made me giggle. "You know it was just last night we were together right?"

She pushed me away just enough so I was at arm's length. She frowned and examined me from top to bottom, seemingly too busy to look me in the eye. I felt a little like a contender in The Westminster Dog Show. "Yes, but when you didn't come by Mary's, I couldn't help but get sick with worry."

I leaned over to give Mary and then Jo a quick hug. "Has she been like this the whole time?"

Mary scoffed. "I hid her keys in case she woke up in the middle of the night and remembered you weren't there."

Jo looked from Mary to me. "Ava woke me up at five a.m., wanting to call you. It took me fifteen minutes to talk her down. In all the time I've known her, she has never been up before me."

Ava, who had been ignoring our discussion to continue her observation of me, finally seemed satisfied that I was unharmed, and we made our way into the kitchen to sit down. We all smirked as she sighed her satisfaction.

"What can I say? I was worried."

I sat next to her and nudged her shoulder. "Aw."

She wasn't amused. "It's unusual for you to go home

to an empty house when the rest of us are all gathered at Mary's."

I couldn't argue her point. "I was going to head over but the thought of a quiet empty house was too tempting to pass up."

Ava shook her head disapprovingly. "Well, I, for one, am feeling insulted. You know I can be a picture of serenity when the situation demands it."

I pressed my lips together while Mary and Jo exchanged doubtful looks with raised eyebrows.

Ava slapped her hands down on the table. "All right fine. Placidity eludes me. But my heart is true. I'm a pal and a confidante."

"Truer words have never been spoken, Ava," I agreed. "Now, if you will allow me two minutes to change. I can tell you what happened."

She nodded. "You have one minute and fifty-eight seconds left."

I ran upstairs and put my hair into a ponytail, tucking my bangs to the side behind my ear. I grabbed the closest top—a black, short-sleeved turtleneck—and threw on some white capri pants. I had just enough time to apply a little mascara and lip balm. I ran down the steps and was sure I had seconds to spare in my two-minute deadline. I sat down, grabbed my coffee, and detailed the events of the night from the moment we parted ways at the restaurant. My friends listened intently to my tale.

"How could someone be so careless?" Ava demanded when I was done.

Mary blew out a breath. "One stupid act and a woman is killed."

Jo shivered. "Talk about bad luck."

Ava leaned forward on her elbows. "Deadly luck is more like it."

I had come to the conclusion sometime between when I went to sleep and when I awoke that I wasn't so sure luck had anything to do with it. "Do you remember in high school—Barbara used to say *what will be, will be*? She called it her philosophy.

Ava nodded. "Yes, everyone else called it obnoxious."

"Exactly," I said. "Because almost everything that happened followed her wishes, whether it was becoming school president or getting a new car for her sixteenth birthday. I remember thinking that her skewed view of fatalism would catch up with her one day. I hate to say it but it seems like her death—being at the wrong place at the wrong time—was fate's way of punishing her for distorting its principles."

Ava looked at me sideways. "That's a ghastly thought, Izzy."

I rubbed my forehead. "I know, and it keeps repeating itself."

Mary looked puzzled. "I hope you're not suggesting anything sinister was at play."

I bit my lip. "I don't know. I just have this bad feeling in the pit of my stomach. It seems too bizarre—impossible even—that an anchor, of all things, dropped from the sky and killed her."

Jo put her hand over mine. "I think you may be getting ahead of yourself. Maybe trying to make sense of something that you can't?"

Mary nodded along with Jo's words. "I agree, Izzy. Who would want to hurt her?"

Ava seemed to be considering the idea, one eyebrow arched and her mouth in an exaggerated pout. "I hate to fuel the fire—well, this fire, anyways—but Izzy has a point. Barbara wasn't exactly a kind or thoughtful individual. A lot of people didn't like her."

I nodded adamantly. "Precisely—and for good reason. She relished in ruling our high school through fear. I don't think she ever changed."

Mary sighed. "I agree that she wasn't the nicest individual—although I only knew her through the club."

Jo raised her hand. "Girls," she said authoritatively. "There's no point in arguing about this until we find out more details. Let's not get ahead of ourselves."

Ava looked impressed. "From timid to tiger. Jo, that newspaper of yours needs to reassign you to the newsroom."

Jo blushed. "I just mean there's a lot of facts we don't know yet."

"You're right," I agreed.

Mary concurred. "So what now?"

Before we had time to ponder the question, there was a swift knocking on my door. It sent a shiver up my spine. Ava, who was sitting closest to the window, leaned forward to sneak a peek. "If there was ever a day to ponder the existence of fate, this might be it."

I rolled my eyes at her attempt to be coy. "For heaven's sake, Ava, who's at the door?"

She gave me a mischievous grin and moved aside for me to look. As I pulled back the curtains gruffly and craned my neck, I was surprised to see a face displaying less patience than I had shown to Ava. I recoiled as Detective Jones looked me in the eye, his brow furrowed and his hands facing up to the sky, likely wondering why I hadn't opened the door for him. I tripped over Mary's leg as I scrambled back and around the corner to where the police officer stood waiting for an invitation inside. I whipped open the door and gave him an apologetic smile as he seemed to search my face for some answer to a question he hadn't yet asked.

Chapter 10

Detective Jones immediately let us know there was no emergency. I invited him in then excused myself to the kitchen where I could gain a little composure and get some refreshments. Armed with a fresh pot of coffee and all the fixings, I felt more relaxed as the detective settled into an empty armchair and helped himself to a cup and a cookie. After a few brief pleasantries, the detective sat back and took out a small notebook and pencil from his jacket pocket.

"So, what are we talking about this morning?" he asked.

We all looked at him quizzically.

His face displayed a faint grin. "Ladies, I have known you all long enough now to be certain of two things. One, when something happens in this town, you know about it. Two, that you have enough insight into the people of this town to make it worth an early morning visit." He leaned forward and grabbed a second cookie. "Besides, I knew if I didn't come here, you'd be surrounding my desk at some point today. This way, I get to surprise you for once."

He then popped the cookie into his mouth and took a sip of coffee.

I exchanged a look with Ava. It was hard not to smile. He had our number. "Detective Jones, I think I can speak for all of us to say we are flattered by your faith in our knowledge."

He nodded in return. Pencil and paper in hand, he jotted something down. Ava tried to crane her neck to see what he'd written. He met her curious eyes head on. "Mrs. Russell, you were at the restaurant last night. I learned this morning that Barbara Wiggins owned a clothing boutique. Based on your proclivity to wear fancy clothing, can I assume you knew Mrs. Wiggins?"

Ava blushed and slowly retreated back to her nearby seat. "Yes, I was there last night and I knew Barbara—both Izzy and I have known her since high school. It's a tragic ending, poor thing."

"That's going back quite a ways," he observed.

"Yes," she replied.

"So, you knew her well?"

"Well enough," Ava said. "We were friendly in our younger days—sorority sisters, in fact. But since college ended, we didn't really keep in touch, other than casual meetings about town."

"And at her store," the detective surmised.

Ava shook her head. "Not often."

He took a few notes then leaned forward intently. "Was there a reason you weren't friends?"

Ava looked surprised at the question.

The detective looked at each of us in turn. "Were any of you friends with the deceased?"

None of us immediately answered. Then Mary cleared her throat. "Detective, I think you've caught us all a little off-guard by your question."

The detective eyed her curiously. "Have I?"

Mary took a sip of coffee. She was rarely flustered, yet seemed momentarily perturbed. Having once been a suspect in a murder herself, I imagined answering questions from the same detective might cause her nerves to fray—just a bit. "Detective Jones, why does this feel like more of an interview than a friendly chat?"

He regarded her with a steady gaze. "Mrs. Whitmore, I'm here because what happened to Mrs. Wiggins isn't sitting well with me. I hoped talking to you ladies about it might offer some clarity."

Jo looked at Mary and then the detective. "In what way?"

Detective Jones closed his notebook. "Off the record, Miss Reynolds?"

Jo nodded, aware he meant away from the prying ears of her employer. "You've got my word."

"Good. I'll get to the point. You see, the weight of the anchor that killed Mrs. Wiggins challenges the idea that this was a simple act of carelessness. Unlike an apple core or a candy bar wrapper, the anchor could not have been tossed over the bridge casually. It would take considerable effort and determination to lift the awkward heavy metal item over the railing."

I slammed my hand down on the coffee table. "I knew it. Barbara was murdered."

The detective cocked his head to the side as he turned his focus onto me. "Mrs. Walsh?"

Ava must've seen my cheeks flush and came to my rescue. "Izzy means that she's having a hard time making sense of what happened last night. Right, Izzy?"

I nodded, toning down my enthusiasm. "I just find it odd that Barbara would be standing at precisely the spot that put her in harm's way when the anchor was dropped. I mean—could that really be a coincidence?"

Detective Jones maintained eye contact with me. "Coincidences of this sort are rare. In the case of Barbara Wiggins' death, I must agree that the circumstances do not add up. It would be virtually impossible for someone not to be aware of the precise location of both Mr. and Mrs. Wiggins. They were under the light, they were talking—I mean, thirty feet directly above them on the bridge. I just can't reconcile myself to accept, at least at this point, that it was a simple accident."

His doubts led me to a hundred questions I wanted to ask. Unfortunately, the detective seemed more eager to pose questions than to answer them.

He wanted to know anything and everything we could tell him about Barbara's character and habits. What became apparent by the time he left was that we knew more about Barbara Wiggins than I realized.

Once he was gone, Ava was the first to grab a fresh cup of coffee. "So, what are we thinking about the detective's visit?"

Mary adjusted her lovely floral scarf, looking more relaxed. "First off, I feel like I owe Izzy an apology," she said, turning to face me. "We know Detective Jones is a thorough investigator and he had the same inclinations Izzy did."

Jo seemed to agree. She grabbed my hand. "Can you forgive us?"

Ava put her arm around me. "Izzy?" she asked. "What say you?"

"There is never a need to apologize for a difference of opinion," I said. "I'm of two minds about the similarities and the inclinations between Detective Jones and myself, of course—flattered on one hand and disturbed on the other. However, more than anything, it inspires me to keep going."

Ava slurped her coffee. "Uh-oh."

I held my hand up. "I just think we could do more—I mean, be more helpful than just a source of background information. As the detective pointed out, we knew Barbara. We also know this town."

Jo grabbed the last cookie. "What are you suggesting?"

A little research seemed warranted. While I had buckets of confidence in the detective's abilities, it was just too close to home to sit back and do nothing. "It would be nice to go back to Cooper's Bridge and take a look around with fresh eyes and daylight."

Jo stood up eagerly. "All right then. Enough said. I need to be home in a few hours. I have some editing to do for my article on fall gardening tips. But I don't want to be left out of this much-more-enticing story. Can I take the role of the herding dog and get everyone up and out the door?"

Ava gauged the room. "Jeepers creepers, why is everyone looking at me?"

Jo put her hands on her hips. "Because no one else takes ten minutes to apply her lipstick."

"But I'm still drinking my coffee," Ava pouted.

Jo peered over. "Your cup is almost empty."

"Haven't you heard? It's good 'til the last drop!"

Jo snagged Ava's cup away and forced our slow-moving friend out of her comfortable seat.

"Do any of you remember when Jo was just a quiet, shy little thing? I'm beginning to miss those days."

Jo smiled. "I'm a newspaper lady now, Ava. A story never waits."

"Good Lord," Ava grumbled sifting through her purse for the aforementioned red stick.

By the time she was satisfied with her reflection and ready to go, we were all in the car waiting. The brunette beauty said nothing as she tied her scarf around her dark curls but managed to stick her tongue out at Jo as she climbed into the back seat of Mary's car, making sure not to smudge her pretty lips in the process.

Chapter 11

It was a short drive to our destination. I could feel my stomach tie in knots as I spotted Cooper's Bridge in the distance. We managed to find a good parking spot along Main Street downtown, right outside the bank, about a two-minute walk from our destination. It dawned on me that the path we were about to follow was likely the same route Barbara had taken with her husband last night—from the bank down to the boat parked along the harbor, where she would enjoy her last glass of champagne then walk until she was dealt the hand of death.

Cooper's Bridge marked the divide between downtown Twin Oaks, on one side, and the less commercial, harbor side, on the other, where the only real destination, other than the marina, was The Mariner's Whisper and a handful of pathways that led to local beaches and parks.

The low-lying structure, used by both cars and pedestrians, crossed the narrow canal that led out to sea. The waterway underneath was not accessible to large boats, which explained why it didn't require much height. But there were proper walking paths along each side.

On the downtown side, the walkway led out to a pier and a small lighthouse. Across the way was where boats regularly docked temporarily. It, too, had a paved walkway along the side that curved around to the Twin Oaks harbor—a skip and a hop away from The Mariner's Whisper.

When we reached the bridge, I walked quickly to the far side, closer to the harbor, and looked over the edge. I guessed this was where the anchor was dropped.

The detective's measurements seemed accurate—it could not have been more than twenty-five or thirty feet above the path where Barbara and Walter were walking. There was a steep grassy hill that reached all the way up to the bridge. One could climb it to avoid the longer, gradual graveled path carved out for public use. I hadn't considered it before, but thinking back to last night, I realized the hill was so dark I couldn't even see it. The light given off by the nearby lamps were not bright enough to light it up. In fact, the spotlight focused strictly at the spot Barbara was killed. Everywhere else remained in the shadows, perhaps giving cover to those not wanting to be seen.

My friends caught up to me, each taking a gander over the edge.

Ava lingered for quite some time, probably because her beautiful long legs afforded her the opportunity to do so without the uncomfortable feeling of the railing sticking in her ribs. "Was it right below here?" she asked.

"Yup, they were walking directly below us when Barbara was hit."

"That's truly frightening."

I peeked over the edge again. Jo and Mary's heads popped out from the pathway below.

"Hello, up there!" Jo shouted.

Ava grinned. "No need to shout. We're within a normal volume up here, even for you, shortstack."

"Can you lend me a ladder? I think I'm going to knock her block off," Jo whispered to Mary.

Ava leaned over even more. "Heard that too, short-stack."

Jo bent down, removed her shoe, and pretended to toss it up at Ava. "Get lost—damned heckler!"

Jo almost lost her balance and Mary quickly came to her aid.

Ava was clearly pleased with herself. "Don't worry, Mary. It's not a big fall. There simply isn't the distance necessary to induce pain."

Jo looked up and shook her fist at Ava. "Let's put your theory to the test. Come on down here. I'll show you how much pain can be induced."

Ava left Jo to put her shoe back on and leaned back to look at me. "I love our little spitfire. It seems like every day she has just a little more sass. I hope in some small measure; I have been an influence on that."

I smiled at her. "Of that I have no doubt. You two have also demonstrated that even the quietest of conversations down there can be heard from up here."

Ava's smiled drained. "Izzy, you know I'm always

your biggest supporter but I'm a little worried you're barking up the wrong bridge."

I bit my lip. "What do you mean?"

Ava looked over the edge again. "Don't you remember in junior year all the highjinks we did on and around this bridge?"

I sure did. "You mean jumping off into the water?"

"That, among other things. It was no secret the whole school called it chicken bridge. For whatever reason, it was a beacon of trouble—leaping over it, drinking under it, there was no shortage of stupid activities kids came up with to pass the time. Have you considered the possibility of Barbara's death being some sort of teen stunt gone wrong?"

I hadn't, really. And she was right. It was a prime location for mischief. "I see what you're saying, but what would they be doing with an anchor? It doesn't make sense."

"Neither does someone waiting in the cover of darkness to murder Barbara Wiggins. I think before you start a list of suspects, you should make sure there was even a crime—at least one with an intention to kill."

Ava had a point. I wrinkled my nose. "I might be getting ahead of myself. It just seemed so clear once Detective Jones came over asking about Barbara's character."

She shrugged. "I'm simply suggesting we do a little more investigating before we start pointing fingers."

I nodded. "Fair enough. And I'm guessing you have an idea?"

Ava stood tall. "Let's go kill two birds with one anchor."

I rolled my eyes. "That makes no sense whatsoever."

She raised an eyebrow. "And yet you know what I mean."

"Only because you so often abuse the English language."

"It's a signature style, Izzy. I take boring expressions and spice them up."

I shook my head and looked around for someone to complain to. Mary and Jo were walking up the steep grass path. "Can someone else sit beside Ava on the way home?"

Ava looked pleased. "I want shortstack."

Jo reached up and swatted at Ava. "You're cruising for a bruising."

Ava giggled. "I just came up with that name today. Now that I see it bothers you, it might have to stick around."

Jo covered her face to hide a smile. "Start walking and stop talking—please."

Ava saluted her. "Yes, ma'am."

Mary took the lead as we made our way back to the car. "Where to, girls?"

I looked at Ava. "Captain?"

"We need to go find us a teenager," she said. "Any suggestions?"

"I have an idea—how about Melanie Humphries? She's only a few years out of high school and I think she might have a younger brother."

Ava frowned. "Are you voluntarily going to visit Jane Humphries, Izzy? I never thought I'd see the day."

I gritted my teeth. "Me neither."

"Chin up, girls," Mary stated. "It's the weekend. Come Hell or high water Jane will be at the club, even if—or rather, especially if—she's heard about last night's tragedy. There is no better source for gossip in all of Twin Oaks."

"Thank goodness," Ava said, as she climbed into the back seat of Mary's car next to me.

Jo turned around and pinched Ava's bottom before she had a chance to sit down. Ava yelped and grabbed her behind. Jo swatted the air and complained about a pesky bee buzzing around. Ava frowned and rubbed the affected spot while the rest of us looked in opposite directions, making sure not to make eye contact, suppressing the urge to laugh. *Quiet retribution had its benefits.* The passing thought sent a shiver down my spine.

Chapter 12

Jane Humphries's house was a place to which I never thought I'd venture. She had a way about her that set off an instinct in me to run. Her desire to be Queen Bee went beyond the average community gossip girl. I had learned over the last few years that if you weren't submissive to her leadership, she would hound you like an alpha dog might bully the runt—it seemed like the same instinctual need to dominate.

Although Jane had grown up in Twin Oaks, our paths didn't cross until a few years ago. We attended different schools and ran in different circles. That changed a few years ago—when I started going more regularly to the Twin Oaks Country Club where Jane, like Mary, was an active member.

It felt very strange this morning walking up the path to her large brick home, surrounded by immaculate hedges and perfectly lined rows of flowers. I was comforted by Mary's assertion that it was highly unlikely the lady-of-the-house would be home, although I still had an involuntary itch to run. Mary knocked and Ava stood tall next to her, ready to pounce if our mutual foe was unexpectedly home. A breeze of relief wafted by as Melanie answered the door, with no sign of her mother to be seen.

The young woman was still in her house robe as she greeted us with a gentle smile. Her attire and puffy eyes told me she must've just woken up. She rubbed her eyes and yawned, apologizing for her state of undress as she waved her hand over her face, as if it might help wake her up. "Good morning, ladies. I'm afraid my mom's not here—she's at the club."

"Hi, Melanie," Ava began. "We wanted to talk to you, actually."

She looked surprised. "Me? Why?"

Ava looked back at me. I stepped forward. "Hi, Melanie. I'm afraid there's been an accident down at Cooper's Bridge."

Melanie's face went pale. "Oh my God—Joey!"

Suddenly awake, she darted back through her house. I realized what she must have thought we were there to tell her, but before I could squash her fears, she was at the top of the stairs shouting his name. I fruitlessly tried to gain her attention.

She charged back toward us. "Where is he? Where's my brother?" she demanded with a panicked expression on her face.

We all began to shake our heads. "Melanie," I said in a calm but insistent way, "the accident didn't involve your brother."

She eyes darted around, examining each of our faces. "I don't understand."

Before I could explain, the door swung open and Joey Humphries came sauntering in, looking and smelling like he had been up to anything and everything but sleep. He scowled at us and looked at the floor, gruffly pushing past us and up the staircase.

Melanie grabbed his arm as he attempted to pass her. "Where the heck have you been?"

The young teen, dressed in all black, minus his cuffed blue jeans, raised his chin to look at her. His lip was curled like a threatening dog. "It's almost creepy how much you remind me of Mom sometimes. Now get outta my way."

He pushed past her, went into what was presumably his bedroom, and slammed the door.

Melanie didn't go after him. Instead, she slowly made her way back down the stairs to where we were standing, looking embarrassed. "Sorry about that. My brother has developed a bit of bad attitude lately."

Mary pointed up at his room. "He's not the first young man to sport a rebellious attitude. Doesn't bother us in the slightest."

Melanie smiled with a big sigh of relief. "Thank you for your understanding. Sorry, I jumped ahead of myself there. What was it that you wanted to tell me?"

I cleared my throat. "I'm afraid we have bad news. It's Barbara—Barbara Wiggins. She was killed last night."

Her face drained of color and expression. "That's impossible," she said searching my face for some sign of tasteless humor or doubt. "I *spoke* to her last night."

My eyebrows lifted as my interest piqued. "What time?"

She shrugged her shoulders and stammered. "It—it was sometime around five, I think. Not late, but she sounded just fine to me. You must be mistaken."

Mary reached out to comfort her but she recoiled from the gesture.

"Melanie," I said softly. "I'm terribly sorry. Unfortunately, I can assure you it is true as we were all witness to the tragedy. I'm sure this must be a big shock."

She stared at me then suddenly started heaving as if unable to breathe. Ava and Mary grabbed her quickly before she collapsed. They each took a side and guided her to a nearby sofa. Ava passed her a nearby pillow. She clutched it desperately.

As her eyes brimmed with tears, she looked at each of us searchingly. "She is—was like a second mother to me. How could this happen? Where did she—she…" Unable to finish her sentence, Melanie covered her face in the pillow and began to sob, still fighting for breath.

Mary stroked the young woman's hair in an effort to calm her. "There was an accident down near Cooper's Bridge just after six."

Melanie looked up the stairs at her brother's closed door. "A car accident?"

"Not exactly," Mary replied softly.

"Does my mom know yet?" Melanie asked.

"I'm not sure," Mary answered.

Ava looked at me sideways. "Although knowing Jane…"

I shot a warning look at her. She didn't finish her thought. Jo crouched down on her knees to Melanie's level. "Do you want us to go get your mom?"

Melanie looked at Jo fearfully. "She's going to be devastated."

"I'm sorry, we didn't realize they were friends," Jo said soothingly, "But your mom is a tough lady. She'll be okay."

"You don't understand. They weren't friends," Melanie explained. "They were cousins. Barbara was the closest thing my mom had to a sister."

Jo looked up at us. "I had no idea."

Mary looked shocked. "None of us did."

She shook her head. "It's okay. Not many people knew. They had a complicated relationship. They hadn't been close in some time but I was hoping to help them reconcile since I was working for Barbara."

I was curious. "Do you mind if I ask why she called you last night?"

She looked at me thoughtfully. "It was odd, come to think of it. Today was supposed to the first day of our annual inventory. All hands on deck type of day. She called to tell me not to bother coming."

"Did she say why?" I asked.

"She said it didn't matter anymore. But when I asked why, she seemed eager to get off the phone. She was distracted."

"Was she upset?" I asked.

Melanie bit her lip, as if trying to stop any emotion from getting out. "Just the opposite—she seemed almost giddy. It was odd."

Just then, the front door swung open. It was Jane Humphries. She froze when she saw us.

Mary stepped forward. "Jane, how are you? We are so sorry to hear about your cousin."

Jane blinked her eyes, looking momentarily taken aback. She scoured the room and crossed her arms, her tight jaw fixed in place. "I appreciate your condolences but would prefer a little privacy, if it's not too much to ask." Jane then turned her attention to Melanie. Her expression softened. "Sweetie, what have you been telling these ladies? You know we like to keep our personal affairs private."

Melanie looked confused. "Mom, they're here to help."

Jane gave her a condescending smile. "Sweetie, these four have a habit of meddling in things they shouldn't. I want them to get out of my house."

Ava looked ready to speak up so I cleared my throat loudly. She must've known the distraction was directed at her, so she rolled her eyes at me but said nothing. Mary was more practiced at diplomacy. She tapped Ava's hand before taking a step toward the door, with the rest of us following her cue. She turned before opening the door. "Jane, you must be overwhelmed with emotion. We will leave you in the capable hands of your lovely daughter."

Jane remained stoic as we each made our way past her, an awkward feat since her stiff body refused to relinquish any ground as to allow us easy access to the exit, she so desperately wanted us to use.

A barrage of fleeting thoughts ripped through my

mind as I walked back to the car, none of which I could say in public without incurring a fine. Mary gently reminded us there was no rule book on grief, obviously sympathizing with Jane's loss, unaffected by her poor manners and rude conduct. Instead of sharing Mary's sympathy, however, I was silently writing my own book on how not to spend a morning—the first rule being never to set foot in that house again.

Chapter 13

With no destination in mind following the Humphries visit, Ava suggested driving by the shop. It was nearby. We all agreed it was a good idea. Normally, this would be the busiest day of the week at the popular boutique. Considering Barbara had died just hours earlier, I wondered if the news had even reached the ears of everyone affected. Barbara spent so little time at the business these days, her absence certainly wouldn't give cause for concern.

We pulled up in front of the shop. It was open for business, as usual. We entered the door and saw a few people browsing. Robin was busy helping a customer, so we all began milling around. A sparkle caught my eye and I wandered over to a rack full of formal wear dresses. I thought I had seen them all the other day, but I realized new ones must have been added in the last day or so. I could have easily chosen two or three others just as pretty as my own recent purchase. Each garment had unique elements that made me appreciate and understand the difference of shopping here as opposed to my usual places. Before I could move on, Robin was at my side with a big smile on her face, obviously unaware of Barbara Wiggins' demise.

"I hope you are here because you want a second dress and not because you have second thoughts," she said.

"I adore my dress. Robin, you have the true gift of style," I replied.

"That's kind, Izzy. Thank you."

"Are you the only person working today?" I asked.

"I hope not. I usually open alone but Melanie should have been here half an hour ago. I'm not sure what's keeping her," Robin explained.

I let out a sigh. "I am. There's something you need to know."

Jo, Mary, and Ava walked over to where we stood. Robin looked confused. "Does this have to do with the weird call from Barbara yesterday?"

"What sort of weird call?" I asked.

"Barbara called me and said the inventory was off— that it didn't matter. I didn't bother arguing, I just came in early to start it anyways. So, I wasn't surprised Melanie didn't come to the designated seven a.m. start, but I figured she'd be in at some point. But now I'm guessing there's more to it?"

I nodded. "Can we step into the change area?"

Ava put her arm around Robin. "I think you need to sit down."

Robin silently agreed by following Ava's suggested

action. Mary and Jo stayed in the front section to keep an eye on the shop, while Ava and I accompanied Robin. Ava pulled the second chair forward so it was across from Robin, and sat down so she could talk to her face to face. "Barbara was killed last night."

"Sweet Heaven above," Robin said, her mouth agape.

She looked to me as if she needed a second opinion before accepting the shocking news. I was standing behind Ava but pressed my lips together and reached a hand out to give her shoulder a squeeze. "I'm sorry."

She stood up abruptly and covered her open mouth. "That is awful. Poor Barbara. What happened?"

"We don't know all the details yet. The police are still sorting it out," Ava explained.

She sat back down and her eyes started to dart around the small change area. Tears began to well up in her eyes.

Ava leaned forward. "If you like, I can stay with you and help out."

She blinked then rubbed her eyes. "I'm okay. You don't need to stay, Ava." Then she stood up again. "I think I need to close the store. It must seem so disrespectful to anyone passing by who knows—knew—Barbara."

I wanted to warn her. "Don't be surprised if the police want to talk to you. They'll probably have a few questions."

Her hands drew up and folded tightly across her chest. "What would they want with me?"

I held my hands up. "I think they are just trying to

figure out what happened. It would only make sense to talk to you—her most loyal employee."

Her arms dropped back to her side. "Yes, okay," she said looking around blankly. "I'd better clean up. I'm sorry to rush you out but I suddenly feel like I can't be here anymore."

Ava stood up and moved the chairs back to where they normally sat. "Of course. But if you need a friend, we're here."

"Sure," she said.

We left the shop hastily. No one else was there and we didn't want to make Robin stay any longer than necessary. She had made her desire to leave clear. After dropping my friends off, I headed home. An urge to nap had pushed all other thoughts and priorities aside. Sleeping during the day had never been a habit of mine, even when the kids were young. But today was different. I was overwhelmed with recent events and the emotional toll felt like it was actually causing my brain to stall.

When I arrived home, I took advantage of the opportune moment. I grabbed my soft wool throw blanket and curled up on the living room couch. The window was open so a subtle waft of the garden lilies floated into the house. Combined with the low hum of my fridge—I was drooling within seconds. I wiped my chin and tucked my face into the corner with the hope there would be no slobber left to clean up later.

I woke with a start to a twilight hue reflecting on the far white wall. Feeling a little discombobulated, I sat up immediately and looked outside at the quiet, empty street. I crossed my hands over my chest and absent-mindedly attempted a soothing shoulder rub—something Frank used to do. Realizing the day had escaped me and I had slept much longer than a standard catnap, I decided I would continue my lackadaisical attitude and treat myself to an oversized, effortless dinner. A drive-in hamburger restaurant had opened up and it suddenly seemed like the only reasonable option.

Although it attracted mostly teen diners, I decided it was the perfect time to relive my youth. All I needed was a partner in crime.

One quick phone call later and I was out the door with a rumbling tummy. Thirty minutes later, Ava and I were pulling up to an open spot.

My enthusiastic friend waved her hand to a nearby carhop. The pretty young woman made her way over and took our orders. We didn't need to see a menu—two cheeseburgers, fries, and root beers, to boot.

Ava turned up the radio. "How have we never done this before? It should be a basic requirement if you have a convertible." She didn't wait for a response. "We seem to fit it pretty well with the youngsters around here, if I do say so myself. I hope we don't actually get mistaken for teenagers. That would be embarrassing."

"Ava, when we were teenagers, the majority of the customers we are surrounded by would still be in diapers. I think we'll be spared any such awkwardness."

She rolled her eyes at me. "You're such a nose-bleed."

I looked in the rear-view mirror. "No, I don't."

"I didn't say you *have* a nosebleed. I said you *are* a nosebleed."

"What?" I demanded.

Ava grinned. "It's teen talk. *Nosebleed* is a term for someone who isn't cool. You've probably heard the term 'drip' or 'square'?"

I shook my head. "I should've come alone. What was I thinking?"

Ava grinned. "You wouldn't dare."

I bit my lip trying to stifle a smile. She was right.

Our food arrived and our conversation halted. I focused on what may have been the biggest hamburger I'd ever seen. I was immersed in its greasy goodness until the last bite, at which point I began to look around at the youthful clientele. My interest was piqued as I recognized a nearby teenager. I sat up straighter to take a closer look. Ava must've noticed. She wiped ketchup from her chin and followed my gaze. "Hey, isn't that..."

I was nodding before she remembered his name. "Joey Humphries—Jane's moody son."

"He looks a little more chipper now, doesn't he?" Ava noted.

I nodded in response but kept my gaze on the now-smiling young man. "You think that flask he keeps taking swigs out of is root beer?"

Ava shook her head. "Considering he conjured up visions of my grandfather as he walked by us this morning, I doubt it."

"Translation?" I demanded.

"My grandfather drank whisky morning 'til night.

Joey had the same distinctive smell. You may not be aware, but olfactory organs are closely linked to childhood memories."

I stopped watching Joey long enough to shoot Ava a sideways glance. "Aren't you a fountain of knowledge?"

She raised her chin proudly. "Bruce ordered a subscription to *Popular Science* for the kids to read this summer. Much to my surprise, I found a lot of the articles really interesting. I suppose I've always had an inclination toward logic and rationale. "

I looked around to see if there was a hidden camera lurking about. "The only thing you learned in science class is that you and Darryl Walker had chemistry."

She giggled. "That we did—although it fizzled out pretty quickly after he lost the school election. He became so moody I found it impossible to be around him. The laws of attraction no longer applied."

I didn't argue her point and instead went back to watching Joey. "Junior over there sure looks better than he did this morning. I imagine it may not be the easiest house to grow up in."

Ava raised her eyebrows. "If you had a mother like his, you'd probably be a little crabby yourself."

I wasn't so sure. "But Joe Senior is always nice. Maybe Jane is a perfect peach at home and just doesn't like us."

Ava scoffed. "Now you're just being obtuse."

I thought about Jane Humphries. As much as I didn't care for her personally, there was always a flurry of activity going on around her so she was a fun person to watch. It was like she summoned worker bees to complete tasks and then report back to her upon completion. Jane's husband, Joe, on the other hand, was much quieter, spending the majority of his time at the club on the golf course or in the Men's Lounge. A retired naval officer, he was definitely older than Jane, although remarkably young to be out of the work force. I had heard he sometimes made feeble attempts at business ventures but never found success, repeatedly abandoning his efforts and returning to his daily life at the club. My few encounters with him were always pleasant, however. He seemed genuinely friendly and very relaxed. I supposed with Jane's driven nature, it was a good fit for them both.

Ava leaned over and nudged my shoulder. "You know, having dated more than a few moody fellas in the past, I've usually found their aloofness comes about when they feel they have been wronged somehow."

I shrugged. "Maybe Joey feels like his parents don't pay enough attention to him. I mean, I've never seen him at the club before but Joe, Sr. and Jane seem to be permanent fixtures. Even Melanie has been busy with school, work, and a new fiancé. Maybe young Joey is acting rebellious to try and drum up a little focus back on him. Causing trouble is a good way to get a parent's attention."

Ava raised her eyebrows. "You're right. Let's just hope a leather jacket and a few swigs from a flask are the extent of his dissent."

Good point. Cooper's Bridge, where Barbara was killed, was developing a reputation for trouble, and sometimes for more than just the silly antics of our youth. Often the dark nooks would be found covered in graffiti and it was rumoured that young men were starting to organize themselves into gangs. At the last town hall, it was brought up as a topic of discussion, with some concerned citizens insisting that a regular police patrol might stop the increase of unsavoury behaviours. I wondered if there was any truth behind the gossip. More importantly, I wondered if any of those young men, drawn to the shadows, was there when Barbara was killed.

After dropping Ava off, I found myself driving back downtown. There was a thought repeating in my head that I had to address. Cooper's Bridge was a place I had crossed on foot more times than I could count—never with any hesitancy or concern. I felt compelled to do it now, determined to prove to myself that that needn't change—there was no bogeyman or evil doer trying to take over my town with murderous intent. I briefly wished I had thought of going there before saying goodbye to Ava, but I dismissed the thought, reminding myself that jumping to conclusions about the bizarre nature of Barbara's death would only give me license to live in fear. I was here to face sinister thoughts and prove to myself they had no place in my head or in my town. And as I approached the quiet destination, I just kept repeating those words, hoping they would sink in before my heart raced out of my chest and abandoned me for good...

Chapter 14

I parked my car on Main Street. Most of the quaint shops that lined the streets were closed for the day. There was a calm ocean breeze coming off the nearby water. As I approached Cooper's Bridge, I looked up at the picturesque vantage point—The Mariner's Whisper, perched just up at the top of the cliffs on the other side. The water flowed gently below, leading out to the small docked boats along the pier and the open ocean a little further down, near the harbor where the larger sailing and motorized boats were kept.

Leaning over, craning my neck, it looked like both sides of the dark tunnel underneath were empty of visitors. Relieved and disappointed, I decided I would walk to the far side and shimmy down the steep hill to take a closer look.

With a little huffing and puffing, I descended quickly, albeit with an absolute lack of grace in my method. I looked down at my peek toe shoes and was glad to see they were no worse for wear. As I looked up, I saw a flash of white and realized I was the object of an onlooker's curiosity. I almost jumped right out of my aforementioned heels. It was so dark in the shadow of the bridge, all I could see was a pair of eyes beholding me with a steady gaze. I took a deep breath and stood tall, trying to emulate Ava's confident stance to alert the person watching me I was no easy target. I didn't bother trying to run back up the hill—there would be no time to escape if, indeed, I was in a situation to which such a response might be warranted. Instead, I waited until my eyes could adjust to the muted light and get a better look at who already had gotten a good study of me.

No doubt a shorter moment than it seemed, I finally got a clear picture of the person standing just a few feet away. It was a young man, perhaps eighteen or nineteen, biting his nails and not looking particularly comfortable as our eyes met.

"Hello," I ventured.

"Hey," he mumbled, not willing to cease his bad habit in order to speak with clarity.

I looked past him down the dark tunnel, where a slew of empty booze bottles, along with a few other young men, were scattered along the lane. They were smoking cigarettes and not looking any more welcoming than the one standing before me—certainly not excited about my unexpected visit.

"What do you want, lady?" the young man demanded. "You here to buy? Sell?"

My mouth dropped open but no words came out.

He began to chuckle and sneer at me as he came

closer, his head down, his eyes up. Before I could think things through, I raised my hand up aggressively. My gesture signaling to stop took him by surprise. I thought quickly. "I'm looking for my nephew," I said in tone matching his.

"Oh, yeah," he sneered. "And who are you, Aunt Gertrude?"

"If I were, my nephew would certainly behave more like a Hardy Boy. Now, you can help me or deal with his mother, who is waiting just up the hill."

He scoffed. "And who might that be?"

"Jane Humphries is her name, and she is—"

He swore under his breath and began to shake his head. "Yeah, yeah, trust me—I know that crazy broad. Came down here last week and threatened to burn the bridge down if her son wasn't home by midnight."

"Did he make it?"

"Hell, yeah. It's not every day someone's mother threatens to kill me."

"Kill you?"

"The bridge wasn't her only target—if you know what I mean."

It wasn't the first time Jane's behavior could be deemed frightful, but I daresay it was the first time I found myself mildly impressed by it.

"So, are you going to help me?" I said.

"No," he said, standing taller and walking closer.

He had a look in his eye that would haunt me for weeks.

Then, before I could say anymore, I heard myself being summoned. My now shaky frame turned slightly to see who had come to my aid.

Approaching from down the pier was Detective Henry Jones. Looking as annoyed as I was surprised, he descended quickly upon us.

"Detective Jones," I began.

His dark eyes glared at me.

The unnamed young man threw his hands up. "Oh, geez, now we got the cops hanging around?" With that, he flipped his stiff leather collar up and spun on his heel, disappearing farther into the shadows and out of sight.

A wave a relief bigger than those hitting the nearby shore washed over me. I tried to feign a casual expression as the police officer led me a good measure away from the underbelly of the pretty bridge. His jawline was tight and he took a few deep breaths.

Curiosity outweighed the sensible notion to remain quiet and wait. "How in the world were you able to see me? I was fully engulfed in the shadows. I mean, when I walked down there, I couldn't see a thing—and that was even before dusk started to fall."

He jawline throbbed and he looked me in the eye. "Mrs. Walsh, you may have just compromised my investigation. I mean, what were you thinking—going down there alone in the dark? I really don't need a second body on my hands—especially yours."

Fighting back tears that had suddenly sprung up, I knew he was right. "I'm sorry." I didn't know what else to say that wouldn't sound like an excuse for my careless behaviour.

He combed his hand through his tousled salt-and-pepper hair. Then rubbed his tired-looking eyes. "I'm going to walk you to your car now, okay?"

I nodded. I decided to stick with the notion to be sensible for the remainder of the walk. It was a quiet one. We took the proper, winding path that led further down the pier before beginning a gradual incline up the big hill. I didn't even look over the rail as we walked back over the bridge. I was trying to show the detective I was not always impulsive and without any good judgement. At least by the time we got back to my car, his jaw was not pulsing.

I paused before getting into my car and thanked him, apologizing for the trouble.

He nodded, acknowledging my words. "I don't need to assign a patrol officer to check up on you until this is resolved, do I?"

"No, and I won't go down there again, I promise. I just didn't think it would present any danger. Not that it did—I don't think…" I trailed off, not sure of my words.

"How about if you get an idea about the case, you run it past me before acting on it?"

I nodded adamantly. "Yes, especially seeing that it is, as you say, a case. I will, promise."

A hint of a smile crept on his face. "Did I say that? Yes, I suppose I did."

His softening demeanor gave me the confidence to ask a few questions. "Have you officially ruled that what happened to Barbara wasn't an accident?"

"Nothing official, no. It's a hunch at this point."

I was certain he was holding back on me. I took a guess. "Anything more on the anchor?"

He studied my face then nodded. "What made you think of that?"

I pressed my lips together as I thought about it. "I guess it's just the most obvious thing that stands out. Our town is chock full of the things, yet I've never heard of one flying off a bridge."

"Interesting." He paused. "The anchor is a puzzle in itself. We have just found out it is a gold antique, reported missing by the marine museum the same day Mrs. Wiggins was killed."

I frowned. "That is odd."

"Yes. It's a one-of-a-kind, apparently commissioned by the king of somewhere or other, a couple of hundreds of years ago, and presented to the captain of a vessel hailing from Twin Oaks. Apparently, the local boat came to the aid of a passing ship that was part of the royal fleet in a nearby storm. Don't quote me on the specifics."

"So, someone stole the anchor from the museum and used it to kill Barbara?"

"I can't tell you what happened with certainty at this point, but it raises enough suspicions to open an official investigation into her death."

"How strange," I surmised.

"Yup. We don't know what, or where this will lead us—never mind the who. The point is that in a case like this we, and in turn, you, must exercise extreme caution. We simply don't know who we're dealing with."

"Of course," I agreed.

"Mrs. Walsh, tell me my words are sinking in."

"Yes, Detective Jones. I promise not to go back under the bridge, at least unescorted—"

"By me," he interrupted.

I raised my eyebrows.

"Or another officer," he added.

I nodded. "I promise."

"There's one other thing," he said, scratching his five o'clock shadow.

I waited for him to spit it out.

"I wondered if you might accompany me to the marine museum. Your knowledge of this town and the people in it could come in handy, considering the complexity of what's happened. This doesn't seem to be a straightforward, open and shut, case."

I stood a little taller. "Should I come by the station tomorrow morning? I can bring coffee."

"Why don't I pick you up, instead? I got the museum to agree to let me look around in the morning. The robbery unit has already been there but I need to see it for myself. Maybe something will stand out."

"Absolutely. I'll be ready by seven."

"If you insist. I'll pick you up at nine."

I agreed. The wary officer dismissed me, and I sped off, my heart and mind racing. It occurred to me only later that there was no way I was anywhere near the speed limit as I waved goodbye to the officer and peeled away from the curb.

Chapter 15

Sunday morning in Twin Oaks was usually quiet. There was little traffic around town and, other than hanging out at the beach, there wasn't much to do. Most shops and services were closed. It was a day for rest and family. I was glad to have plans that got me up and prevented boredom from setting in.

On days I knew my family and friends were busy, I sometimes found myself getting into my car and driving to the city. Less than an hour's drive, New York was a place bustling with activity on practically every street corner. I loved getting a fresh cup of coffee and wandering the streets to see what people were up to. Frank used to wonder if my love of coffee was due, at least in part, to its natural, heart-pumping effects. Fifth Avenue was one of my regular haunts. The wide avenue and the energy made it always a fun place to wander. I loved looking at the window displays and watching who had gotten all dolled up to go shopping. Then there was the hustle and bustle of Times Square—people and cars going in every direction. It was fun trying to guess where each passerby was headed and what made it such a rush.

Before I had time to make a second cup of coffee, Detective Jones pulled up in the driveway. I grabbed my scarf and headed out, not wanting to make him wait or come up to the door. He asked after my family and I explained where the kids were what they were up to. It made me realize I didn't know anything about his personal life.

"Do you have much in the way of family?" I asked lightly, trying not to come across too nosy.

"A little," he answered.

"But you're not married—I think you mentioned that before."

"Did I?" He seemed a little surprised.

"Yes."

He looked over at me. "I work too much to dedicate myself to anything or anyone else, I'm afraid. I try to keep my life simple."

I nodded and dropped the subject. If I wanted to stay in his good books, I figured I'd better zip it.

We arrived at the museum a few minutes later. It was at the end of a dead-end street, where an empty gravel parking lot was set up to accommodate visitors. It looked like an old brick home that had been converted to its current status, but it was kept up nicely and had a very welcoming feel. The front door, which I assumed would normally be kept ajar during opening hours, was shut. I wondered if anyone was even inside. The detective gave a swift knock at the door and shortly after it was opened by a vaguely familiar looking face. It was rather dark inside so it took a minute for my eyes to adjust. Once they had, I still couldn't immediately place where I knew the man standing before us. He was tall and thin, about my age, and had light hair and dark eyes. When the detective introduced himself and me, I stood there scratching my head.

The man's eyes lingered on me, even as Detective Jones held out his hand to shake. The man took it but even as he did so, his locked gaze remained. The detective must have picked up on it, as well.

Detective Jones cleared his throat to recapture the man's attention. "I'm sorry, now that you know who we are, perhaps you could introduce yourself. We didn't get your name. I was only told someone would be here to greet us."

"Sorry, Detective," he began, looking the detective in the eye briefly before returning his focus on me. "I'm just surprised to see this friendly face before me—one who I must say, hasn't aged a day since high school. My name is—"

My mouth opened with surprise and recognition all at once. "Darryl Walker."

He smiled, obviously pleased I recognized him, too. "You remember."

"Of course I do—we did spend four years together at Twin Oaks High, right?"

His smile faded. "Don't remind me." He must've detected the dismay spread across my easy-to-read face. "Of it, not you. I'm happy to remember you, Isabelle.

May I ask if you still see Ava? I still think about her, you know. She was like a beacon of light for me during some dark days."

My cheeks flushed and I suddenly felt uncomfortable. I wasn't certain whether my happily married friend would want me discussing her with an old boyfriend. Luckily, Detective Jones seemed to pick up on it and share my discomfort. "You two can reminisce when I'm not on the clock—and preferably when I'm not in earshot. Sentimentality is not my cup of tea."

Darryl scoffed. "Believe me, Detective, Twin Oaks High doesn't warm my heart much either. There are few people I wish to remember and fewer memories still." The palpable bitterness made me cringe.

The detective pressed along with his agenda and didn't bother to remark on Darryl's final comments about the high school days we shared. But the harsh feelings he displayed regarding our time together at high school stayed with me for the remainder of our visit. However, I told myself to push it aside. I didn't want it to distract me from the reason I was here.

Darryl was very knowledgeable and helpful regarding the stolen anchor. He went into great detail regarding the history of it. It was a tale full of heartbreak, compassion, and heroism. A local fishing boat braved a storm after recognizing a distress symbol from a much larger, foreign ship that had been badly damaged. Although much of the crew was lost, the dozen or so saved made the local men heroes—both at our home and at theirs. The royal family of the European country who owned the merchant boat were so thankful to the captain and crew who saved the survivors, especially given that one of the men saved was their youngest son, they had the anchor designed and hand-made, arriving a few months after the incident occurred. Given that the anchor was originally meant as a symbol of thanks for saving lives, I found it sad and ironic that it had been used in such a tragic manner to end one.

Darryl seemed very pleased that the missing object would be returned next week. It was funny thinking back to the valuable piece—I wondered whether the person who used it to kill Barbara knew its long, dramatic significance or whether it was just a means to the end of her life, accidentally or otherwise. Was there some sort of connection that we were unaware of that could link the anchor, or at least the theft of the anchor, to her death?

The detective asked if there had been any other recent break-ins or items gone missing that they hadn't reported before. Darryl seemed confident there wasn't but promised to check with the rest of the staff in case he'd missed or forgotten anything. The detective wanted to know whether there were other valuable items in the museum and what sort of security the museum used to house and protect such items. He seemed reluctant to admit there weren't many. The anchor had been in a locked display case, but the thief could have easily picked the simple mechanism to get it out without making much of a ruckus—it wasn't like the museum was chock full of security.

Detective Jones was not one to linger. After getting

the rundown on basic facts and taking a few minutes to look at the housing for the anchor, he stated we had all the necessary information we needed and promised Darryl he'd be in touch with the museum as soon as the anchor was ready to be picked up. He suggested a review of the security measures might be something for the museum to consider. Darryl agreed he would add it to the upcoming budget review in the fall.

Darryl led us back to the entrance. He hesitated before opening the door to bid us adieu. "Detective Jones…" he began, obviously at odds with himself whether or not to continue his inquiry.

Detective Jones seemed to pick up on Darryl's uncertainty. "Mr. Walker, if there is something you need to ask or tell me, now is the time."

Darryl stammered. "I normally don't inquire into business that isn't mine. However, I can't help but wonder why the police sent a detective instead of a constable to ascertain the facts surrounding a reported theft. It strikes me as a little odd."

"You seem quite familiar with police procedure, sir," Detective Jones commented.

Darryl looked at him proudly. "I spent a number of years in the navy—shore patrol."

"I see. Those must've been some tough years. Thank you for your service," Detective Jones said. "To answer your question, yes, normally a constable might be the first point of contact if it were only the anchor we were interested in. However, it has been linked to a serious offence that requires more in-depth investigation."

"May I inquire as to what that was?" he asked.

"I'm not comfortable discussing the facts just yet. However, I will disclose that a woman was killed and the anchor was found near the scene."

Darryl looked from the detective to me. "What are you telling me? The anchor was used to kill someone?"

"I am not at liberty to discuss an open investigation," the detective stated. "We should be going. Thank you for your assistance."

Darryl acquiesced.

"I'll meet you at the car?" I asked Detective Jones.

He gave me a warning look. "Be quick Mrs. Walsh. I don't have all day."

I promised. The detective left. Darryl looked at me curiously.

"I felt like you should know, at least, who was killed," I said.

He raised his eyebrows. "Do I know them?"

"Yes, I'm certain you do. It was Barbara Wallace. Her married name was Wiggins."

He blinked repeatedly, pulled his lip down, and shook his head. "Doesn't ring a bell."

I found myself blinking a lot, too. I knew he was lying. I just didn't know why.

He went back to smiling. "If you see Ava, please let her know I said hello. I will always cherish the time I spent with her. On dark nights at sea, I used to pretend the brightest star was lit by her, sending me a signal that I'd be okay—she was there to guide me. I just wish she—I mean, it—would've stayed with me upon my return home. It's strange, you don't always see the darkest moments coming, do you?"

The car horn beeped and I jumped.

Darryl reminded me the detective was waiting. I stumbled through an awkward goodbye and hurried outside.

I turned to take one more look at the museum. I hadn't been there since Darryl and I were classmates. I walked back to car slowly, as the vivid memory came rushing back. It seemed like fifteen days ago, not fifteen years—a field trip for history class. At the time, I was less concerned with what the museum had to offer and more interested in the nearby beach. I slipped out a side door and hustled over to catch an hour of afternoon sunshine with a few friends, Ava and Darryl among them.

Ava never spoke much to me about Darryl. Perhaps because we weren't as close back then, or perhaps the feelings he had were never shared by her. Either way, I needed to find out more about my old high school classmate.

Barbara had torpedoed Darryl's reputation when he ran against her for class president out of anger and spite. I decided before getting back into the car, I was not ready to do it again by sharing unsubstantiated questions and concerns with Detective Jones about him.

Why had Darryl pretended not to know Barbara? Did he harbor ill will toward her? Could he be capable of committing murder because of unresolved resentment and hate going back fifteen years to high school? It was a quiet ride back as both the detective and I mulled over our own thoughts on the mornings outing.

Chapter 16

I had been anxious to speak to Ava. She was one of the most popular girls at our high school. When she and Darryl dated, they were the golden couple—fun, friendly, and attractive. But when Darryl ran against Barbara Wallace in the school election senior year, everything seemed to change. He lost the vote and subsequently seemed to fade away from school life. He and Ava broke up around the same time and I couldn't seem to remember much about him after that. I hoped Ava could shed light on the details of what happened to him, and if his rivalry with Barbara was a part of his fall from grace.

Barbara was part of the same popular crowd as Ava, but she wasn't nearly as friendly or nice. While Ava's popularity seemed natural and easy, Barbara's felt calculated—she was aware of her status and clung to it using control and fear. No one could argue that she was very pretty, but her manipulative and bullying manner were in direct contrast to her outer beauty. However, she seemed to be loyal and friendly to those she felt worthy, and thus maintained a friendship with Ava that lasted throughout our high school days. While they didn't remain close following graduation, Ava was always happy to see Barbara and would reminisce about their days together at Twin Oaks High.

I wanted to know whether the seemingly pivotal events that tied Darryl and Barbara together could possibly lay the foundation for a resentment that could fester into hatred powerful enough to serve as a motive for murder.

Something else was bothering me. I felt terribly guilty about not sharing my knowledge about the strained relationship between Darryl and Barbara with Detective Jones. I worried it would catapult Darryl from a helpful and willing source of information to a possible suspect. Considering we did not even know, at this point, whether Barbara's death was a tragic accident or the result of premeditated murder, I wasn't willing to cast a doubtful and suspicious eye on Darryl, nor did I think it fair of the police to—it just seemed premature. Unfortunately, my justifications did little to assuage my conscience of its burden.

I grabbed my keys and drove. Two minutes later, I arrived. So much for clearing my mind on the open road. Ava's husband, Bruce—or as I liked to refer to him, Clark Kent's long-lost twin—opened the door. He gave me a big smile and looked relieved. "Thank goodness you're here."

I looked at him curiously. He called over his shoulder to Ava, instructing her to unstrap herself from the ankle breakers, and come to the door. Odd visions began to fill my head. I frowned.

He sighed. "Just wait—you'll see."

Ava clamored up the basement stairs with such heavy footsteps, I initially wondered if they were not-so-secretly housing an elephant. Then I saw what was attached to her feet—she was wearing shoes with metal wheels at the bottom, each shoe bearing four wheels underneath, attached by leather straps that tightened over top. Her expression told me the exercise was not going very well. I had a sense of déjà vu.

I looked at her. "Should I even ask?"

She huffed. "Those young girls at the restaurant yesterday made it look so easy—rolling around, fetching orders, looking cute. Well, let me tell you, it is not cute. It is awful. I haven't even attempted to leave the house yet."

Bruce quietly steadied her as she attempted to sit down on the nearest seat. "I think you've done enough for today, hon. Why don't you two go out and have a little fun? Hopefully it won't prove to be as difficult or dangerous as roller skating—although I suppose with you two it's always hard to say."

Peering around, I wondered, "Where are the kids?"

Ava smiled. "One look at my latest purchase and they ran out of the house quicker than I could get the straps on—said they were too young to witness a fatality."

Bruce nodded. "They did have plans with their friends, albeit a little later. But now you two can go do something and I can cut the grass in peace, without having to worry about broken bones and head injuries."

Ava tossed the roller skates in the front closet, where they would likely remain until covered in dust and properly forgotten. She then took a few minutes to powder her nose and kissed her prince good-bye. Before I knew it, we were en route. To where, I wasn't sure. But with my best friend in tow, it never seemed to matter. Without a doubt, my day was looking up.

"So, where to?" Ava asked.

"Good question. The only requirement I have is a place that can accommodate discreet conversation."

She raised her eyebrows. "My, my, Izzy. What do you get up to when I'm not around?"

I ignored her cheeky insinuation. "Maybe we should just drive and talk. It certainly ensures discretion."

She shook her head. "Unacceptable. If my stomach is empty, which it is, my ears get distracted by the grumbling of my tummy."

"You remind me of Katherine—when she was five."

She stuck her chin up in the air. "You daughter has always been very intuitive. Thank you for the compliment."

An idea struck me. "Why don't we stop by the bakery—it's open until noon today. We can grab some baked goodies and drive up the coast?"

"You'll hear no argument from me. The salty breeze will do us good."

We grabbed an assortment of fresh treats from the bakery around the corner and headed out. We were in no hurry and took our time cruising up the coast. We savored the moment—and the sweets—focusing on the warm ocean air. We passed the beach and looked over at the number of people enjoying the day with friends and family. It brought me back to why we were out. "Do you remember our high school field trip to the marine museum in senior year?"

She puckered her lips and squinted her eyes. "Okay, yes. That's when Darryl tried to impress me with his athleticism and ended up almost drowning. A big wave hit him close to shore and he swallowed a gallon of water. He was coughing for hours."

"Wasn't that because you donned your bathing suit right on the beach?"

She gave me a cheeky smile. "I was wearing it under my outfit and it was getting hot. I didn't know it would almost kill the poor guy."

"Didn't you?"

She took a bite of her chocolate covered donut and swatted at me. "Oh, c'mon now, you know I'd never wish him harm, as moody as he proved to be. I hate to say it, but that day may have proved to be a highlight in our relationship."

I shook my head as I thought of the outmatched young man. "Was Barbara Wiggins there, too?"

Ava clicked her tongue as she remembered back. "Of course, like the majority of our class. The teachers must've noticed the dwindling attendance at the museum."

"Oh, probably," I agreed. "But it was near the end of

the year. They probably didn't feel like chasing us all down."

She grinned. "You're right. What made you think of that day? It seems like ancient history now."

"I saw Darryl this morning."

Her jaw dropped. "What? You're teasing."

"I'm not. And it's probably the first time I've seen him since high school."

Her eyes were still wide. "That's because his dad made him join the navy straight out of high school—he was gone right after graduation."

"Wow, was his dad in the military?" I asked.

She shrugged. "I don't know. But I *do* know it was because Darryl lost to Barbara in that stupid school election."

I frowned. "I don't get the correlation."

Ava raised her eyebrows. "Losing to a girl?"

I thought back. "I guess he did get teased a bit."

"More than a bit—but worse than that was the reaction at the factory where his father worked. Apparently, after shooting his mouth off about Darryl's guaranteed victory, he felt utterly humiliated when Darryl lost, blaming it on laziness and a poor work ethic. It drove him to pressure Darryl to join the navy—to make a man out of him, so he said."

I frowned. "I thought Darryl was more interested in art and history."

Ava scrunched her nose. "He was. It was not a mutual decision. The worst part was he never even wanted to run for school president in the first place. The principal insisted on it—desperate to avoid having to deal with Barbara in charge of the student body. He told Darryl that if he didn't run, he'd be benched from the football team for the whole season."

"Geez, that's tough."

She nodded. "Yes, but not as tough as being pressured to enlist. Darryl was distraught—he only did it because his dad threatened to disown him if he didn't."

"You were broken up by then, weren't you?"

She raised her eyebrows. "We had broken up months earlier, but after that stupid election, Darryl's friends turned their backs on him. He was the laughing stock of the football team. He had no one else to talk to except yours truly. What made it worse was Barbara's relentless teasing of him. Before that, I thought of her as a good person and a good friend. But seeing the way she tormented Darryl made me realize how unkind she really was. When I asked her to stop, she told me to stop worrying about my loser ex-boyfriend and lighten up. I was never able to see her again in the same way."

I scoffed. "Sounds like you finally saw her the way the rest of the school did—enough said."

Ava sighed. "I guess you're right. Where did you see him anyways?"

"At the marine museum. He works there now."

"What? Wait—isn't that where…" Ava didn't finish her thought. We both recognized the implication—she just connected the item used to kill Barbara with someone who may have a motive to want her dead. A now familiar thought crossed my mind. *Could a high school grudge from fifteen years ago hold enough venom to cause someone to strike?*

We drove for a while in silence. It was impossible to be sure whether Darryl had a legitimate motive to kill Barbara without knowing more about his life after high school. It seemed Barbara's humiliating treatment was directly linked to the events following his graduation. If he was successful in his endeavors, there would likely be no lingering resentment, I supposed. However, if it led to difficult or unhappy years in the aftermath, it might be enough to consider Darryl as a suspect, assuming the police concluded Barbara was the victim of foul play.

I was ready to tell Detective Jones what I knew and leave the rest to him. Although I could see the look of concern on Ava's face, I reminded her of how effective Detective Jones had been solving crimes in the past. I was certain this would be no different. She seemed reassured by my words and we spent the rest of the afternoon enjoying the summer sun with the top down and the past behind us.

Chapter 17

As we coasted back into town, a small window sign caught my eye. There was a *For Sale* sign hanging in the now empty window of Barbara's Closet. I pulled over to get a better look. Ava looked around to see what had prompted me to stop.

She raised her shades. "Sale?" she asked excitedly.

I scrunched my nose. "As a matter of fact, yes. But it may be more than you have in mind."

I pointed to the sign in the window. She looked at me in horror. "Say it isn't so."

My eyebrows furrowed. "It can't come as too much of a surprise."

Ava walked toward the store. "The word surprise doesn't cut it. This shop has been here for years—I'm flabbergasted. With Barbara's passing, I assumed Robin would take the reins again. For all intents and purposes, she was back in charge anyways. It doesn't make sense."

I peered in the window and saw some movement inside, despite the closed sign hanging on the door. "Why not ask her yourself. It looks like she's there now."

Ava nodded and began knocking on the door impatiently. A moment later, the door swung open. But it wasn't Robin, as we assumed it would be. Standing before us was Melanie Humphries. She smiled at us sadly and invited us in.

I gave her a quick hug. "I hope we're not intruding."

She shook her head. "It's nice to see a few friendly faces. It feels so quiet and solemn in here now. A week ago I loved spending my days here—today, I've been here twenty minutes and I can't wait to leave."

Ava stepped forward. "Is there anything we can help you with?"

Melanie sighed and slumped against a wall. "I appreciate the offer but I don't even know where to begin myself."

I looked around. A few racks were empty, but otherwise it still looked orderly. "What exactly are you trying to accomplish?"

She threw her hands up. "I wish I could tell you."

Ava looked hopeful. "There's a sign in the front window that implies the store is closing. Did we make the wrong assumption?"

"No, you got it. The store is shut down but it's a complicated situation. I'm trying to stay neutral but it's getting ugly—fast."

I frowned. "What do you mean?"

She looked around. "I shouldn't really be saying anything but my mom told me the bank is trying to back out of some deal they had with Mr. Wiggins, and it sounds like it's getting personal. Robin and I are treading lightly—she won't even set foot in here until it's resolved for fear of getting dragged into it. But I thought maybe if I could organize the shop, it would help ease the tension."

I was confused. "So, Walter is fighting with the bank?"

Melanie bit her lip. "It's really none of my business but apparently just before Barbara died, there was some agreement made to pay off the debt the shop had accumulated in exchange for an early lease termination. Since Barbara is now dead, Mr. Wiggins wants to wait until the insurance money is paid out and the bank refuses to extend the terms."

Ava's nose wrinkled. "Geez, that does sound ugly."

I began to wonder. "What about Robin? I can't believe she wouldn't want to pick up where she left off?"

Melanie looked distraught. "It's not that simple, I'm afraid. The bank is no longer willing to do business with the shop at all, no matter who is in charge. Fortunately, in that regard, Robin seems as uncomfortable as everyone else to even set foot in here since Barbara's death. It's suddenly lost its appeal—it can never be the same."

I conceded. She had a point. Tragedy had clouded the boutique's charm.

Ava was frowning. "Melanie, how does your mom even know all of this?"

She blushed. "Mom is friends with one of the senior clerks at the bank. She pressured her friend to find out what was happening since it could affect me."

Ava regarded Melanie with sympathy. Then she rubbed her hands together. "You know I've spent a lot of time in this shop. I'm sure I know it well enough to help sort through the clothes—organize the inventory, if you think that might help."

Melanie looked hopeful. "Really?"

Ava and I both nodded. The young woman looked at us thankfully. "That would be really great—thank you. Maybe if we can sort the clothes out and repackage them, they could be returned and refunded."

I nodded. "There must be thousands of dollars in merchandise here. If the suppliers are in any way nervous about getting paid, I'm sure they'd be much happier to have their goods returned than run the risk of a total loss, even if it's not their normal policy."

She looked pleased. "My fiancé had similar thoughts. I came down here determined to help. Then I got overwhelmed."

Ava smiled sympathetically. "Well, your fiancé sounds thoughtful and practical. Good qualities in an accountant."

Melanie beamed with pride. "That he is."

I stretched my arms out and looked around. "All right, ladies, it's already getting late. Let's talk as we work."

Ava shook a fist in the air. "Make haste, girls. No one can tell me I am not an efficient worker."

I paused to look at her. "Except when the foreman did—at the munitions factory. He must've said it at least once a day."

"It's an expression, Izzy."

I grinned. "I'm not so sure it is."

She stuck her tongue out at me. "Just be quiet and do your job." Then she kicked off her heels and yawned. "Why don't I go make some coffee?"

Melanie and I looked at each other and giggled.

By midnight, we had the store inventoried and organized by supplier. The clothes were packed in cardboard boxes we found tucked away, and the store now looked like it was ready to rent. Looking both tired and sad, Melanie and Ava didn't argue when I suggested calling it a night. Melanie told us she could call her brother to pick her up but we were happy to drive her home. I hoped our efforts would provide some comfort to those closest to Barbara.

I dropped Ava off, took a deep breath, and looked forward to tomorrow. The morning sunshine would chase away the heavy darkness, which was beginning to envelop me on this cloudy, starless night.

Chapter 18

I awoke feeling energized and full of purpose. I had compiled a mental list of things to do and was ready to get at it from the moment my eyes were opened. I was determined to see if there was anything else I could find out about Barbara's death. My day would begin with a trip to the bank.

It was curious that the bank would be so unwilling to compromise or renegotiate a deal for terms regarding the closing of the business, considering the main player had just died. I wondered if Melanie had some of the facts wrong. I also wondered, if it was true, why Walter wasn't willing to just pay what was agreed upon in the first place. There was no doubt he could afford it. I knew one of the full-time bank tellers at the bank, Nora Rogers, and hoped she might know what was going on.

I walked through the door to the bank just after it opened and was surprised to find it busier than usual. People were bustling around—mostly staff. I spotted Nora quietly sitting at a small desk in the back, and

walked toward her. Nora was the wife of a mechanic em-
ployed by my husband, Frank. When he died, she and a
few others regularly brought pre-made meals for me and
the kids, just to help out. They kept it up for months. The
thoughtful gesture made a remarkable difference. Grief
seemed to temporarily freeze my insides, from my emotions, to my brain, to my body. Having help with simple
chores, such as cooking, took a huge pressure off me to
be prepared and organized. I knew I would never forget
their kindness.

When Nora saw me, she stood up and opened her
arms. "How's my favorite boss?"

I smiled. "Oh, please."

Nora shook her head. "Just because you're not running the show doesn't mean people forget." She gave me
a squeeze. "It's good to see you, Isabelle."

"You too, Nora," I returned.

I would never get used to thinking of myself as the
head of a company. It's not like Frank even prepared me
for the possibility. Luckily, he and Ava's husband,
Bruce, had gotten things organized for the unlikely sce-
nario of Frank's early death. When it all came to be, I
wasn't even aware that Bruce worked tirelessly to put the
plan in place and secure my future. Bruce specialized in
business accounting and helped Frank turn his one shop
into several then organized the expanded business so it
ran like clockwork, including preparation for the worst-
case-scenario. Frank never shared that with me, so when
Bruce came and explained how it would all work, not
long after the funeral, I hesitantly agreed, putting my

trust and faith completely in Bruce to sort it all out. He did an amazing job, finding men to run the business that were both trustworthy and willing to work for a company now owned by a woman. While I rarely got involved, Bruce still watched over it, and I was fortunate enough to draw a generous income with the profits. One of the measures in place to keep the business running smoothly was to ensure the employees, from the top down, were paid generously to minimize turn over and keep the staff happy. Nora was a prime example of its success.

"Izzy?"

I looked at Nora who seemed to waiting for me to speak. "I'm sorry, did you ask me something?"

She grinned. "Did you forget to have your morning coffee? You seem a little distracted."

I returned her grin. "I suppose I am."

She shook her head. "I was just wondering what I can help you with."

"Well, actually—"

Before I could finish my sentence, Bob Cole, the bank's manager, came storming out of a nearby office. Everyone froze. He breezed out the front door and everyone around seemed to let out a collective sigh of relief before getting back to their tasks at hand.

I looked at Nora. "That was odd."

She looked at me sheepishly. "You know Mr. Cole?"

I nodded.

She leaned in closer to me. "Well, if he was unpleasant normally, he's downright awful today."

My nose wrinkled. "Yikes."

There was almost no one in Twin Oaks who didn't know Bob Cole—he ran the only bank in town. Unfortunately, the power seemed to go straight to his head and he was easily one of the least liked men around. I had met him years before when he was a financial advisor at the bank that Frank and I went to ask for a mortgage. The first thing I noted about him was the determined scowl that never left his face, as if it was below him to speak to someone who needed a loan in the first place. I remember thinking about how much Mr. Cole looked like a weasel. Since that day, the image was conjured up anytime I saw him. I was never quite sure whether it was his close-set eyes, his round, old-fashioned spectacles, or his long, pointy nose, but one would be hard-pressed to deny the resemblance. On top of that, his voice was unusually high and he regularly tapped his index fingers together, as if silently clapping for every penny the bank earned.

I shuddered at the image and focused back on Nora. I seemed to tune back in mid-sentence. "…the regional manager is on his way unexpectedly."

"Is that why Mr. Cole is more out of sorts than usual?" I raised my eyebrows, finding it hard to believe there could be such a thing.

She giggled. "You got it. Trust me, around here, it's never a good sign."

I let out a long whistle. "Oh, dear."

"Exactly. There's been some intense meetings here recently with a top client. I wouldn't be surprised if that's the reason for the visit from the brass."

Her words triggered a thought. "You wouldn't be

talking about Walter Wiggins, would you?"

I caught her off-guard. She looked worried. "How did you know? I didn't mean to give out confidential information."

I shook my head. "Don't worry, Nora, you didn't. I actually wondered if you might know why Mr. Cole is so opposed to negotiating the terms of the sale from Barbara Wiggins's shop."

She looked even more surprised still. "How did you even know about that?"

"I don't even know—let's just say someone let it slip. So, it's true?"

She tilted her head toward me. "I shouldn't comment about Mr. Cole's decisions, but everyone around here is scratching their heads about it. I have a feeling head office might share our doubts. He's been obstinate about everything to do with that shop ever since it ran into trouble a few months back. I don't think Barbara Wiggins and Mr. Cole liked each other very much. But I really can't say any more. You understand."

I nodded adamantly. "Of course."

She looked around at the bustle before looking back at me. "I'm sorry, Isabelle. I haven't even asked about why you're here. What can I help you with today?

"Don't worry, Nora. It looks like you have your hands full. I'll come back another time. Besides, you may have helped me more than you know."

Nora looked a little wary as I gave her my warmest smile and bid her good-bye.

Chapter 19

I walked out of the bank with a spring in my step, feeling rather proud of myself for confirming further details surrounding Barbara's death. Outside, my peppy walk came to a screeching halt when I spotted Bob Cole in a tete-a-tete with a taller, more pleasant looking man. He wore a nice suit and had bright eyes. Their conversation, exchanged in almost a whisper, was obviously intense. Mr. Cole's gaze never wavered, but I guessed from the sneer on his lips, poorly covered by an awkward grin, that he was not fond of the topic, the man to whom he was speaking, or both. I was compelled to move just a little closer, pretending to look across the street while keenly eavesdropping on their private conversation.

It was Mr. Cole who I heard first. "…I am the manager of the bank, let me remind you. That position affords me a wide discretionary field in which to do business."

The unnamed man huffed. "Mr. Cole, it's bad enough when you refuse to consider ideas to save a sinking ship. It becomes absolutely unacceptable when you refuse to negotiate with one of our most valued clients. And speaking of value, you may want to consider what your position at the bank means to you."

I was standing so close to Mr. Cole, I could almost feel him shaking with rage.

"I may not have a cousin to boost me up the bank's mighty ladder, but I have dedicated my life to this place. I will not be manipulated by a woman who wants to play games. I stand by all the decisions I have made. Women do not belong in business. Barbara Wiggins made that abundantly clear. So don't you come in and tell me how to run things around here. I'll do it my way."

The victim of Mr. Cole's verbal assault seemed unfazed by his vitriol. Calm as a cucumber, he leaned over Mr. Cole's trembling figure and paused. Then he purposely looked down at the much shorter man and smiled. "You can do it your way, of course, Mr. Cole. However, the way you choose to behave will have consequences. Either fix this mess immediately, or start looking for a new position."

Mr. Cole didn't respond with words. Instead, he spun on his heel, almost knocking me off the curb, and stormed back inside. Luckily for me, the man he had been speaking to quickly came to my aid, reaching for my arm before I fell into oncoming traffic.

He swiftly stabilized me on the sidewalk and withdrew his arm. "Pardon me, ma'am. I must profusely apologize for that gentleman's conduct."

I looked at him with an embarrassed smile. "Gentleman?"

He raised an eyebrow, obviously surprised by my offhand remark. "Good point. It rather gives those of us who strive to be so a bad name."

I brushed myself off. "Too bad your manners have less effect than your words. It seems you've really upset that man."

He grinned at my offhand comment. "Yes, unfortunately, when you are scolding someone who believes they are above reproach, they tend not to appreciate the polished manner in which the words are delivered."

My embarrassment was eased by his good nature. "A suggestion from the president himself would unlikely be welcomed from prickly Mr. Cole."

He looked surprised. "I must apologize. I didn't realize you were familiar with the man in question. I misspoke."

I shook my head. "On the contrary, I think you summed him up perfectly. But don't worry—we are not friends and our paths rarely cross, thankfully. Your words will not be repeated."

He grinned. "You are a fresh breath of air. I appreciate your discretion, Mrs...."

I held out my hand. "Isabelle Walsh."

He took my hand and gave me an appreciative nod. "You are a breath of fresh air, Mrs. Walsh. Thank you. I'm Grant Marshall."

I looked up at the fair-haired, moustached man. "Nice to meet you, Mr. Marshall. I wish you more pleasant conversations in your day ahead."

He grinned. "That wish has already been granted,

Mrs. Walsh. But it is a lovely sentiment, and I shall keep your warm thoughts with me for the remainder of it."

I beamed at him and said good-bye, pleased with the insight I had gained. I sensed it was just the beginning of a day to get things done.

Chapter 20

It was a quick drive to my next destination. When I arrived, the white drapes in the large front window were all still drawn. I wondered what sort of state Walter Wiggins would be in. I approached the large, two-story white Georgian home. It had meticulously manicured bushes surrounding it and a flawless lawn. I thought it a shame there were no flowers to brighten up the somewhat austere look, but supposed a colorful garden wasn't for everyone.

A formal and rather grim housekeeper opened the door. I asked to speak to Mr. Wiggins. She had me wait and excused herself. Upon her return, she reluctantly welcomed me into the front foyer and disappeared.

Mr. Wiggins soon came into sight. He looked remarkably changed from the few times I had met him before, and certainly not the way I expected. He bobbed up and down with a light step—rather surprising given his large, round frame—and a friendly grin. If I had not known better, I'd have guessed he was just back from a relaxing vacation, not a widower of only two days.

I tried to return his grin but it likely came out a little wilted. "Hello, Mr. Wiggins," I began. "I just wanted to stop by and check in."

He tilted his head to the side, his lips pressed into a toothy smile, and his eyes crinkled. It was rather disconcerting. "That is very kind of you, Mrs. Walsh. But please, call me Walter."

I nodded in response, as I struggled for my next words. "Thank you, Walter. Might I inquire as to how you're managing?"

He invited me to sit down. I thanked him and took a seat on the nearest option—a stiff blue velvety chair, shaped like a seashell. He sat next to me on an equally stiff settee with the same design. If the goal was to make me feel welcome, it did not work.

Walter didn't seem to notice. "I appreciate you coming to check in on me. Had you been here yesterday, you would've found a man not unlike the one you assisted the night of my wife's untimely demise. I struggled for a long time. It may have been the longest two days of my life, in fact. But I woke up this morning from a deep sleep and felt the sunshine on my face—it was like God reassuring me that Barbara is okay now—finally at peace. So, I am listening to His message and following suit."

I was confused. "Was Barbara suffering before she passed?"

He looked at me incredulously. "Well, if you knew her at all, you'd know the answer is yes. You see, Mrs.

Walsh, Barbara was always angry at someone—usually me. Anger in itself is a form of suffering. Now that she's gone, I've stopped cowering. I can't even remember the last time I woke up and felt relaxed, knowing there would be no critical eyes or words targeting me. I've gained an inch already. I see it as a parting gift from her."

I couldn't hide my shock. He must've noticed my reaction. He held his hands up defensively. "Don't get me wrong, Mrs. Walsh. I miss her terribly, of course, but life does move on."

I forced my head to nod. "Yes, yes, it does."

He furrowed his brow. "Perhaps now that she has passed, she will even find joy in the afterlife. I mean let's face it, she was never Miss Congeniality."

I could think of nothing to say.

Walter looked out the window in an attempt to look forlorn, I assumed. A moment passed and he stood up abruptly. "I hate to push you out. But I'm afraid I have somewhere to be and I must get going. You know they only serve breakfast until eleven at the club. Will I see you at the funeral on Tuesday?"

I stood up. "Yes, I'm sure it'll be a full house."

He looked at me dubiously. "Perhaps. Well, thank you again for stopping by."

I said good-bye and left. I didn't start the car right away because I needed time to allow my mouth to shut after the shock of the conversation forced it into a perfect, gobsmacked O. I didn't want to catch any flies, after all.

Chapter 21

Detective Jones was standing at his desk with his coat on when I arrived at the police station following my strange visit with Walter Wiggins. Before I had a chance to ask for him, he saw me and came over.

"Good timing," he said, leading me back to the entrance. "I was just on my way out. Care to join me?"

I paused. "Can I ask where you're headed before agreeing to go along?"

He chuckled. "I suppose you can but I'm a little short on time. C'mon, I'll explain on the way."

I followed him out and into his car, hopped in, and waited patiently to find out where we were going. He drove out of the station and insisted I fill him in first, aware I was not one to leave well enough alone. As I began to explain my whereabouts over the last day, Detective Jones was his typical self, not asking too many questions, instead just listening quietly until I seemed exhausted of things to say. It was very effective. I ended up prattling on, as per usual, as if he was silently pressuring me to do so, including everything I knew about the conflict between Barbara and Darryl Walker in high school.

When I finished, he gave no reaction other than a nod and subsequently informed me we were heading back to Barbara's Closet to look around and talk to Robin Manners whom he had spoken to earlier that day on the phone, to ensure her presence at the shop. I was a little surprised, based on what Melanie had told me—that Robin was staying away from the store to avoid any conflict or drama. Then again, I knew how much Robin cared, and I supposed it made sense.

We pulled up to the shop and saw the now-familiar for sale sign posted in the window. The lights were on and I was pleased to see Robin inside. Detective Jones tapped lightly on the window. She looked up and approached, unlocking the door and welcoming us inside. Robin was dressed much more casually than I had seen her before. She was wearing black clamdiggers, a floral top, and rosy ballet flats. It was something I could see myself in, although maybe not with the same bold color scheme. Robin was obviously busy. Although cordial and friendly, it was obvious she was distracted. Since I had spent considerable time helping Melanie at the shop only yesterday, I was able to determine that she must've gone through a variety of goods. We had organized the inventory in a basic manner, keeping the dresses sorted from the skirts, tops, etc. Robin had two stacks neatly placed on the counter but there was a bunch of stuff that must've come from re-sorting each pile from yesterday's effort.

The detective asked if there was anywhere to sit. She led us to the back section where there were enough chairs for the three of us.

Detective Jones pulled out his notebook and flipped to a new page, retrieving a pen from his shirt pocket. "Before we start talking, I want to make sure you're okay with Mrs. Walsh being here. I invited her along as a friend. She's helped me out in the past and I figured in a place like this, I might need a little guidance. I'm not accustomed to being surrounded by women's apparel."

Robin nodded and looked from him to me and back at him again. "Of course, that's no problem. Izzy is always welcome here. I'm not sure what I can tell you, Detective, but I want to help in any way I can. Barbara was good to me."

Detective Jones didn't say anything. He just looked at her, as if waiting for her to expand on her answer. I was relieved to see he didn't just do that to me. I looked away, feeling awkward, but remained silent to respect the detective's method, assuming that's what it was.

Robin scratched her head. "Yes, I mean, Barbara was good at delegating tasks and allowing me, in particular, a huge amount of freedom to basically run the store as I pleased."

He frowned. "That sounds like an awful lot of responsibility."

Robin nodded. "It was. But I loved it. I'm not sure if Izzy told you, but I used to own the shop."

Detective Jones looked up at her as if searching for meaning in her assertion.

She smiled. "I was young and ambitious. In fact, I was at the bank so much—pleading with them to trust me with a loan, I ended up falling for the banker who approved the money. Two years later, we were married. I then sold the store to Barbara. When my marriage fell apart, I needed a purpose and Barbara needed a manager. She took care of the bills and I did the rest."

"Did she pay you fairly?"

"I didn't do it for money. I did it because I loved it. My divorce settlement left me well taken care of."

I wondered, "What are you going to do now, Robin?"

She looked at me sadly. "I don't know. I'm still trying to come to peace with what's happened."

The detective tapped his pen on his notepad. "My understanding was that Mrs. Wiggins didn't spend much time here."

Robin shook her head. "She didn't, really. Three or four hours a week, at most."

The detective paused. "Mrs. Manners, were you aware the shop was in trouble financially?"

Robin held her hands up. "I was in the dark about all that. Barbara never involved me. As far as I knew, things were good. We had strong sales, busy as ever. I don't know the figures, but when I owned it, it was stable and profitable. I don't understand it, to be honest."

Detective Jones took notes and nodded. He pressed his lips together. "Okay, and as far as staff goes, was it just you and Mrs. Wiggins?"

"And Melanie Humphries. She's part-time but a

great asset, as well," Robin explained proudly.

He made a note. "One more question, Mrs. Manners. Have you seen any men hanging around the shop, maybe looking in the windows? Someone you didn't know or someone Mrs. Wiggins knew that made you feel uncomfortable?"

She closed her eyes and her brow furrowed in concentration. A moment later, she gasped and looked from me to Detective Jones. "There was an odd moment last week. Barbara was about to walk into the shop. Right in front of the door, a man accosted her. I couldn't hear what was said but she seemed to know him and was quite shaken up. When I asked her about it later, she said it was just some creep from high school. She passed it off like it was no big deal. Maybe she was wrong. I can't say I've ever seen Barbara that scared. I'm sorry I didn't get his name."

The detective frowned. "Could you describe this man?"

She nodded. "He was unremarkable looking, to be honest. Rather tall and quite thin. He had blond hair, I think. Other than that, I couldn't really say."

It sounded an awful lot like Darryl Walker, although I supposed the description could fit nearly half the men in our town.

Detective Jones scribbled notes in his pad. "Would you recognize him if you saw him again?"

"I think so, yes."

I had to butt in. "Robin, have you seen the man since?"

She shook her head.

The detective pulled out a pen and wrote down his number. "If you see him again, call the station immediately. Do not approach him or let him know you even recognize him. Do you understand?"

Robin looked worried but quietly agreed. The detective thanked Robin for her time and we left the shop. As we drove back to the station, the detective's face remained strained. I had a feeling I knew why. "A penny for your thoughts?"

"The vague description given by Mrs. Manners matches only one individual tied to this case."

He was right. "This is where things could get very dangerous. I trust you not to get involved any further."

I put up my hand, ready to swear on the Good Book.

He pulled up to a traffic light and scanned my face. "This is one lead and it could go nowhere."

"*But…*" I implied.

"But it could lead us to a murderer. From here on out, you must not share anything you've been privy to— even with your best friends."

"Of course," I promised.

"Good."

We arrived back at the police station and Detective Jones thanked me for my time and insights. I bid him good day and drove home. I hoped I hadn't just sealed the fate of an innocent man.

Chapter 22

I had been in and out so often lately, I decided to take the morning off poking around and work on my garden, instead. It was lovely outside, and I often found the peaceful surroundings of my garden a great place to think—it was quiet with floral scents wafting through to keep my senses keen yet relaxed. I heard the telephone ring a few times but didn't bother to rush inside to answer it. I figured if it was that important, the caller would try again later, or stop by in person. Likely, it was just Ava checking in, which she did routinely every day.

I was trying to obey the orders of Detective Jones by staying completely out of his investigation.

By now, I knew there was no doubt in Detective Jones's mind that Barbara Wiggins had been murdered. He never came out and said it conclusively, but having been around a few of his cases in the past, I had no doubt he was certain her death was the result of a sinister action.

I tried to think of a hundred other topics that would

normally occupy my mind quite contentedly, such as my children, current events, and the latest movies coming out.

But I couldn't stop my thoughts from continually going back to who would want to harm Barbara and what the motive could be.

Before I had any answers to my questions, I heard the squeak of my backyard gate opening. I turned to see Ava rush in, looking quite dismayed at my current occupation. "What in the world are you up to? I've been trying to call you for hours."

"It's nine a.m."

"I got up early."

I grinned. "Should I drop off a copy of my daily schedule on your doorstep?"

She seemed to be seriously contemplating my offer when I walked over and swatted her. "Well, what is it that you needed to tell me so desperately?"

She grabbed my gardening gloves and tossed them aside, leading me back inside as she gave me a wide-eyed knowing look. "There's been an interesting turn of events. Mary heard from one of Jane Humphries tennis friends that Joey Jr. has been arrested."

I frowned. "Arrested?"

Ava nodded. "Apparently, Jane was on the golf course when she got a call from the police station. She left fuming, telling her golfing companions that heads would be rolling once she straightened things out, declaring her son was no criminal. Mary called me when she couldn't get in touch with you—assumed you'd want to know after Joey Jr.'s little show the morning after Barbara's death."

"Do you know what he was arrested for?"

Ava shook her head. "No, but I called Jo at the newspaper and asked if she could find out. She didn't promise anything but said she'd look into it."

I was impressed. "Good thinking"

She raised her chin and smiled proudly. "Thank you. I told her I'd head over here and we'd wait for her call. I even wore practical shoes, just to be speedy."

"Aren't you clever," I teased, taking a peek at her ballet-style flats. "I wasn't aware you still owned any."

"I keep a pair on hand for just such emergencies."

I smiled. "How practical."

"It is, isn't it? I must be maturing," she said with a sigh.

I patted her shoulder. "Let's not get ahead of ourselves."

I was about to make a fresh pot of coffee when the phone rang. It was Jo. She informed me that Joey Jr. had been arrested at a pawnshop downtown trying to sell stolen items. She didn't know any more details, but would let us know if she found out. I thanked her and hung up. The phone rang almost as soon as I had hung up. This time, it wasn't for me. Ava's husband was calling to remind her they had a tour booked at Twin Oaks Country Club—at Ava's insistence. She listened quietly, her ear pressed next to mine, then swore under her breath, obviously having had forgotten about her previous priority. I quickly relayed to Ava what Jo told me and, reluctantly, she left. We promised to meet up as soon as she was back.

Just as I had put my gardening gloves back on, the doorbell rang. I assumed it was Ava again, likely having left something behind in her hasty departure. The incessant knocking was a dead giveaway.

But I opened the door to discover my error and an unexpected guest. Standing before me was Melanie Humphries. As soon as she saw my face, she broke down into tears. I ushered her in.

There was little doubt as to the reason for her sorrow. My heart went out to her. "I heard your brother is in some hot water."

She looked up at me and nodded. "How did you know?"

I pressed my lips together and widened my eyes. "Small town."

A long sigh escaped her body and it seemed to deflate her fragile frame. I removed my gardening gloves and led the young woman to my couch. Without hesitation, I excused myself long enough to brew a pot of hot tea. It seemed to have more soothing properties than its caffeinated counterpart. She took it gratefully. I waited quietly while she had a few sips. When she put the tea down and looked ready to talk, her tears had stopped and she seemed a little calmer.

"Sorry to barge in on you like that."

I dismissed the apology with a wave of my hand. "My door is always open to you, Melanie. Now, tell me how I can help."

She had another sip of tea as if it would bolster her confidence. "How much do you know about my brother's...situation?"

"I know he was arrested trying to sell something that didn't belong to him."

"That's why I wanted to talk to you. He hasn't been formally charged yet—they let him go, but told him to stay close by. I know you have helped the police before, particularly when they are looking in the wrong direction, so to speak. I hoped maybe you could help my brother, too."

"Are you telling me he didn't try and sell stolen property?" I asked, doubtfully. Joey didn't have a squeaky clean image.

She cast her eyes down and shook her head. "No, that part I don't doubt, unfortunately. It wouldn't be the first time he's been in trouble like that."

I frowned. "Then what is it? What do you think the police have got wrong?"

"They keep asking questions about our family—about Barbara."

"Barbara?"

"Barbara Wiggins, you know, my mom's cousin."

"Yes, I knew who you meant, Melanie. But why would they be asking Joey about her?"

Melanie's jaw grew tight. "It's the stuff he tried to sell. You see, Izzy, it's all stolen junk from the marine museum."

I sat back. *Could it be?*

"That's not all," she confided. "You see, my brother

has sworn to the police that he just found the stuff near Cooper's bridge yesterday..."

"And you don't think he's telling the truth?" I asked.

"Izzy, you're going to help me—help my brother, right?" Melanie demanded. It was the first time I had seen a glimmer of her mother in her character.

I shook my head. "I'm not sure, Melanie. If you're brother hurt Barbara—"

"No, he would never hurt her. I'd stake my life on it."

I nodded, having full confidence in her sincerity. "I will try to help find the truth—wherever it leads. How about that?"

"Thank you, Izzy. That's all I ask."

I was relieved that my promise calmed her frazzled nerves. "Good. Now you need to tell me everything—including whatever your brother withheld from the police."

She audibly blew out all the breath she had been holding. "Okay. So, my brother told the police he found all the items down near Cooper's Bridge, under some bushes. He admitted he should've alerted the police but tried to sell them instead. That's the first lie."

I raised my eyebrows. "Only the first?"

She nodded ever-so-slightly. It made me worry. *What could be more incriminating than being in possession of items related to the murder weapon?* I didn't want to get ahead of myself so I stayed on point. "How do you know it was the same stuff?"

She rubbed her lips together. "After you left my

house the other day, I went to my brother's room. I found him putting the stuff in a secret hiding spot my mom doesn't know about. He didn't hear me, so I kept quiet. A few minutes later he went for a shower. I sneaked back into his room to see what he was hiding. I thought it was just a few trinkets—some old rusty old junk I assumed he found on the beach."

"What else did he lie about?"

"Just one other thing."

"And that is?"

"Where he was the night Barbara was killed."

"Did he tell the police he was home?"

She nodded.

"And you know he wasn't."

She continued to nod. "I hadn't seen him in two days. You, Ava, and the other ladies were there when he got home. It wasn't unusual for him to stay out late but that was the first time he didn't come home at all, at least that I'm aware of."

I wasn't surprised to hear he'd stayed out that night. After all, the combination of whisky and salty air nearly bowled us all over when he walked through the door and sulked past us. But it hadn't occurred to me that it could be in any way related to Barbara's death. Until that very moment.

I was beginning to regret my decision to help Melanie. Not because I wouldn't want to—but the idea of giving this lovely young woman a false sense of hope when the truth didn't seem to allow for much, was worrying. No matter how desperately she wanted her brother to be innocent, no amount of digging could change the facts.

"What was Joey's relationship like with Barbara?" I asked.

"It was strained. He had been moody for months. I don't know anyone he actually got along with lately."

"Was there something going on with him? Something that had been weighing him down?"

She shook her head. "Nothing specific, as far as I know. He just had an attitude lately. He complained about society, spouting all sorts of garbage about doom and gloom. It was really quite annoying, to be honest."

"Okay."

Melanie sighed. "Izzy, he pretended to be tough and wanted people to think he was some sort of rebel, but I promise you, he is a good kid. He cares about our family—and that included Barbara. You know, she used to be over all the time, when we were younger."

"What happened?"

"It's complicated. She and my mom went through cycles of liking each other then hating each other. The latest cycle of their feud had been going on far too long but it doesn't change how they felt about each other. And that goes for Joey, too."

"Did it bother your mom that you were working for Barbara?"

"It drove her crazy. She hated that I was spending more time at Barbara's store than at home. But I hoped it could help mend their relationship. It's one of the reasons I took the job there to begin with."

"I understand. Family can be complicated. Let me see what I can find out, okay?"

She pressed her lips together and smiled. She believed in me. A lack of motive was a beacon of hope I intended to rely on. If everything Melanie told me was true, Joey could be involved in something way over his head. Getting into trouble might have him thinking that lying to the police was his only option. I needed to find out how he had really come into possession of the missing items and where he was the night, the moment, Barbara was killed. He might be hiding details that could lead to the truth. I needed to earn his trust and show him the truth may not be as scary as whatever or whoever he was afraid of. Fear was the only rational explanation I had for him lying—that was, unless Melanie was wrong and he was the killer himself. But for now, I'd leave that theory to the police, as I guessed the young man had raised enough doubt to have made himself a possible, if not prime, suspect.

I wanted to talk to Joey Jr. as soon as I could. Melanie called home to get an update on his whereabouts. When the police let him go, Jane had taken him home, made him shower, then insisted on them going to buy him a new wardrobe, as if different clothes would change his attitude. Melanie figured Joey and Jane would likely be getting home soon, if they weren't there already. She was right. Her dad told her they were just pulling into the driveway.

I knew this was my opportunity. I wasn't sure how I'd convince his mom to let him talk to me, but I guessed even Jane would sacrifice a personal bias against my so-called meddling if she thought there was the smallest chance I could help her son. She may not be the most likeable person in the world, but I would never count her for a fool. I didn't doubt the love she had for her children outweighed her pride or her love of privacy, no matter how much it pained her. Melanie agreed and I followed her back to her house in my own car. I wanted access to a quick getaway in case Jane chased me off their property.

Chapter 23

As we pulled up to the Humphries' residence, I pinched my arm discreetly to make sure this wasn't a bad dream. I certainly did not anticipate coming back here any time soon after my last visit. However, seeing that a young man's future was at stake, never mind the truth behind a woman's death, I reminded myself a side of humility with my fresh cup of coffee was well worth the trade.

Melanie smiled nervously as she opened the door and welcomed me inside.

I told myself to live by Ava's rule—grabbing onto even the lowest rung of confidence was a great start to climb the ladder up. I was holding on with all my might. It was a good thing, because as I took my shoes off, bony red-painted toes were planted squarely in front of me. No need to guess who they belonged to. I slowly stood up and purposely rolled my shoulders back. "Hello, Jane."

"Isabelle, please tell me you are here to sell cookies for one of your tearful charities."

"Actually, my good will is focused on your family today."

Melanie, who had walked ahead to likely look for her brother, grabbed her mom's arm. "Mom, I asked Izzy to come. I trust her. Joey is in trouble and she can help. You know she has helped the police before and can influence the direction they take."

The description Melanie gave her mom was not one I appreciated. "Melanie, I wouldn't go so far as that. But, as I told you earlier, I'd be happy to talk to Joey if he's up for it. I'm aware of his troubles."

I could see Jane struggle with herself. "If I allow my son to talk to you, do you promise not to spread a word of what's been said to the neighborhood gossip gang?"

I had to refrain from a snappy retort. "I won't tell my friends what we discuss, if that's what you mean. But anything I learn today, I must share with the police."

"Against my better judgement, I'll allow it. God knows we're desperate at this point. Come on in, Isabelle. I'll get my son."

I purposefully bit my tongue and followed Melanie into the living room, where she apologized quietly for her mother's tactless manners. I nodded in return, not particularly thrilled with hers, either.

I could hear an argument ensue, then Joey entered the room guided by his mother's elbow. Joe, Sr. was standing right behind them. He smiled meekly, looking like he wanted to be anywhere but here. I knew how he felt. I smiled awkwardly. "Hi, Joey. I'm Isabelle, you can call me Izzy."

"What do you want from me?" he asked directly.

Melanie stepped in before I could answer. "Joey, Izzy is here because I thought you'd be more comfortable talking to her than to the police. She's really nice and she can help."

He shook his head dejectedly. "No one can help me. Just leave, lady."

His mother pulled him farther into the room and directed him to sit across from me. "He's here now. Talk."

Joey looked up at his mom then curled his body into a small "C" shape with legs dangling out the bottom. I wondered if I'd ever felt so awkward or out-of-place.

Joe, Sr. came into the room and asked Jane to go make coffee for me. When she began to argue, he looked at her sternly and she reluctantly left the room.

He sat down beside Joey and put his arm around him. "Son, I don't need to tell you that we're in some trouble here. You're a good boy who has made some mistakes. I know this lady well enough to tell you she's a kind person who might be able to lead you to the light. I'm no good at this stuff and your mom isn't either. Talk to her—for me, son. I'll keep your mom occupied for as long as I can." Joe, Sr. stood up and looked down at me. "Thank you for coming. Melanie told me she was going to ask you to come here and I encouraged it. My wife means well, but she's upset and my son is scared."

I appreciated his words and it gave me the encouragement I needed to reach out to Joey. "What do you think, Joey? Should we have a chat?"

He uncurled and looked at his father then me. "Let's just get this over with."

Joe and Melanie left us alone and closed the French doors that separated the room from the rest of the house. I tilted my head and bit my lip. "Joey, what your family said is true. I'd like to help you."

He sat back. His young faced looked strained. "I don't even know what to say. I know the police think I hurt Barbara. I would never, ever hurt her. I…" He couldn't finish his sentence, his emotions took over and he started to rub his eyes and his forehead in an effort to stop it.

"I've lost someone I loved, too. It's awful. I can't imagine if people thought I had been the cause. Do you want to tell me about the stuff you tried to sell?"

"I told the cops—I found it."

"I know that's what you said. But I also know it's not true. Your sister saw it in your room."

His face flushed and he cursed. I waited passively for him to process what that meant. "I didn't kill her."

I believed him. The hurt on his face was raw. "But you do know more than you told the police."

He didn't argue.

I took a different approach. "Can you tell me why you took that stuff? Did you need money for something or was it just for kicks? Believe me, I did some things when I was younger I'm not proud of either. I'm not here to judge you."

He intertwined his fingers and put them behind his head. "Things got out of hand. I was just…just letting off steam, I guess. I don't even know why I did it."

"What was it about the museum that drew you there?"

"I don't know."

"Was it the anchor—the one that killed Barbara? Did you know its value?"

"What? No, I didn't want to do that. He made me do it. I just meant—" He stopped talking. It must've dawned on him he'd said more than he wanted.

I sat up. "Who? Who are you talking about, Joey?"

He shook his head. "No."

"What are you worried about? Did he threaten you?"

His mouth was open wide and his tongue was fidgeting around. He looked nervous.

"Joey, whoever this person is does not have power over you unless you let him. The police can protect you. Don't let some thug intimidate you. We're talking about your future."

He threw his hands up. "Don't you think I know that? I'm trying to protect my family. He could destroy us."

"Whoever *he* is, is lying. No one has that power."

"You have no idea."

"Okay, how about this. Can you tell me what he asked you to do, without telling me his name? That will at least start to make sense of why you're covering for the potential murderer of your aunt."

He sat back again and closed his eyes, straining them shut to stop the tears welling up. "I was being stupid, trying to be cool, with a few of my friends. I had gotten some fireworks and we were setting them off in an alley downtown. One of them hit a store window and it cracked. That led to picking up some rocks and finishing the job—"

Joey stopped to gauge my reaction. I was unfazed. He continued. "I moved onto nearby cars—breaking a few windows. He saw us and started chasing us. My friends got away but he caught me when I tripped on the sidewalk. I knew who he was. He recognized me, too. That's when we both knew he had me."

"What did he want?"

"At first I thought he just wanted to scare me—he was furious because I smashed his precious car window—or at least that's what I thought. He told me I could go to jail. I didn't care. Then he told me I'd start caring once my parents suffered the consequences. I froze. He knew he had me and I knew he could do it, too."

I wracked my brain for who he could be talking about. "What did he want you to do?"

"Nothing at first. Then he called me a few days later. I met him down near Cooper's bridge. He told me I was going to make up for my family costing him everything."

"What did he mean?" I asked, hoping that might help me identify the man.

"I have no idea, even now. I broke one lousy car window."

"What did he tell you to do?"

"Break into the museum. He told me to steal that damned anchor—the anchor that killed my aunt. If I didn't take that stupid thing, she'd still be alive."

I looked hard at the young man. "Was it Darryl Walker?"

He shrugged his shoulders. "I don't know."

I was confused. "I thought you knew who it was."

"I know what he looks like, not his name."

"Is it the man in charge of the museum? Tall, blond, and thin."

He shook his head. "The only way to describe that chump is to show you a picture of a weasel in a fancy suit."

I balked. "Bob Cole?"

A booming knock on the door made both of us jump.

Chapter 24

Joey and I rushed to the door, getting there just seconds after the rest of the Humphries. It was just in time to overhear Detective Jones demand to know where Joey was. The young man looked at me and began to tremble.

Judging by the intensity in the detective's voice, he had reason to. I stepped forward with Joey behind me, as Jane demanded to know what he wanted with their son.

Detective Jones looked from her to me to Joey. His expression didn't change. It was impenetrable. "I need to know where Joey was after he left the station this morning."

Jane looked at her son. "I took him straight to Donaldson's Men Shop on Main Street to pick up some respectable clothing, then we came back here. You told us not to allow him out of our sight. The only time my eyes have left him is when Isabelle demanded time alone with him."

The detective's eyebrows raised up, just slightly. "Mrs. Walsh?"

I rolled my eyes. "While I might argue about circumstances, the bare facts are correct. Joey and I have just been talking for the last thirty minutes or so. Aside from that, I have no doubt of what Jane is saying. Her motherly instincts demand she be with her son after the events of the last day."

It was the closest Jane and I had ever come to being allies. The detective sent away the two officers accompanying him. He looked at Joey. "You're a lucky young man to have these two at your defense."

Joey said nothing. I feared the worst. "Please tell us what has happened, Detective Jones."

He ignored my question. "Might I come in, Mr. and Mrs. Humphries?"

Jane waved him in. He took a seat in the same room in which Joey and I had just been talking. I sat next to the detective and the Humphries filled the remaining seats. "I'm afraid there's been another death in town."

I frowned. "I'm guessing you're here because it wasn't by natural causes?"

He nodded. "That's correct."

Jane huffed. "Oh great, my son has gone from a thief to a murderer now?"

Melanie gasped. "Mom, stop."

Joe, Sr. cleared his throat. "Detective Jones, please continue."

The detective surveyed the room. "The reason I'm here is because I believe there is a correlation between Barbara Wiggins's death, the theft at the museum, and now the death of Twin Oaks' latest victim."

156 Lynn McPherson

I couldn't wait. "Who is it?"

"Bob Cole, Twin Oaks Bank manager."

Joey Humphries made a strange gurgling sound. He may have almost choked on air. The detective looked at him and he looked at the ground.

Jane didn't seem to notice. "What on earth made you think to come here?"

"It was something left at the scene, Mrs. Humphries."

"What kind of thing?" she demanded.

He cocked his head to the side as he addressed her. "Something that tells me your son may not be guilty of this gruesome crime, but he certainly knows more than he's admitting—at least admitting to me." The detective paused to give me a stern expression before looking back at Jane. "You see, Mrs. Humphries, deep down in Mr. Cole's fancy suit pocket lay a small piece of paper with the initials J. H. and your phone number written on it. Now, do you have any more sharp-tongued questions for me now, or can we try to be a little more civil from this point forward?"

She kept quiet and asked no more questions.

That gave the detective the chance to delve deeper into the recent history between Joey and Bob Cole. Detective Jones took advantage the effect his announcement had and used the obvious fear that Joey was experiencing to get him to open up.

It was a smart move—Joey was singing like a church choir on Christmas morning. It was fairly repetitive of what he'd just told me.

As I listened to Joey's story a second time, one glaring question began to nag at me. I waited as patiently as I could until he was done.

I was as calm as wafting lavender in the summer breeze while Joey talked, making sure not to get in the way or interrupt, so it surprised me, when he was done, that Detective Jones then turned to me and asked if there was something I wanted to add.

I frowned. "Why do you ask?"

He pressed his lips together and pointed subtly to my foot. I looked at it as if it belonged to someone else. It was jiggling up and down like a jackhammer and I looked at him apologetically. I hadn't noticed it moving.

"Sorry," I said.

He nodded congenially and was about to speak when I blew out a loud breath.

He stopped again. This time he just scratched his head. I knew I had better speak up before he lost his patience. "I'm sorry to interrupt, but I just can't help but wonder when and how the anchor came into the possession of the killer—or at least when Joey lost possession of it. I think I'm missing something."

The detective nodded and looked at Joey. "Only one person can answer that. Can you enlighten all of us? Don't skip the details."

"It was the day Barbara died. Mr. Cole called me and told me it was time to make up for everything we had cost him."

I held up my hand. "Who did he mean when he said 'we'?"

Joey shrugged his shoulders. "I didn't ask questions. I just wanted to get it over with."

"Sorry," I mumbled.

"He told me the museum was closed and to go inside and get the anchor—that it was in the back room in a big display case—I couldn't miss it."

"That's it?" the detective asked doubtfully.

"I asked how and why. He said since I was smart enough to break car windows, I shouldn't have any trouble. Other than that he told me to mind my own business. Said to meet me with it just at six under the bridge."

"What happened?"

"I went early, around five and it was like he said—the museum was closed. I jimmied the lock on the side entrance and went in. It was creepy, I didn't linger—I smashed the display case the anchor was in and grabbed it—plus a few doo dads, since I was there anyways. Then I left. The thing wasn't exactly inconspicuous so I hustled over and stashed it in some bushes, at the top, where the bridge starts. Then a few friends of mine passed by—asked if I wanted to hang out. I figured it was hidden good enough and had almost an hour to kill. Besides, I was twenty feet away from the thing, just under the bridge having a little sip of this or that."

The detective sat back. "Are you telling me someone found the anchor in the bushes while you were goofing off with your friends nearby?"

Joey threw himself back against the sofa, looking frustrated. "Yeah, I guess I am. It sounds stupid but I don't know what else could've happened."

Detective Jones leaned forward. "Any chance Mr. Cole could've taken it?"

He shook his head. "No, he was with me when..." Joey stopped talking and pressed two fingers hard against his forehead.

Jane stood up and gasped. "Joey—you saw Barbara being murdered and didn't do anything to help?"

When he looked up at his mom, there were tears in his eyes. "I froze, Mom. Then I called out to her, then Walter—no one heard me. I wanted to run across, swim across, anything, but that creep, Cole, grabbed my arm so tight his nails left bloody prints in my skin. He said to keep my mouth shut or he'd kill me. He wasn't a big man, Mom, but he scared me." Joey stopped talking and started sobbing. His mother ran to him and held her son in her arms, trying to soothe his shaking frame.

The detective gave the pair a minute then cleared his throat loud enough for them to know the questions weren't done. Joey looked up again, now with his mother's arm wrapped tightly around his shoulders.

Detective Jones was impossible to read. There had been no change in his demeanor. He maintained a keen focus on Joey. "I need you to close your eyes and think back. After the anchor dropped, did you see anyone around, anyone walking, running, strolling, even crawling off that bridge?"

Joey closed his eyes and we all watched his face twist with emotions as he replayed the scene in his mind. "No, I mean, not really. When Walter picked Barbara up and walked away with her, we all just ran—including

Cole. I don't remember the next few minutes, other than just running. The streets were busy, the shops were just closed—people were still everywhere. It's like I just couldn't get away. Then I went back—I had to know if Barbara was okay. I knew he must've taken her to the restaurant so I went there—looked in the window. I saw Mrs. Walsh—" He pointed to me. "—and Walter and then the cops showed up. I ran to the only place I knew I could hide—back to the tunnel. I watched you all come back with Walter, but I was where I had been, on the other side, and I just couldn't face it. I found some friends and started drinking. I woke up the next morning on the beach and went home. It all seemed like a bad dream. Until I saw Mrs. Walsh again and knew it wasn't. It was like Mrs. Walsh was my conscience, showing up everywhere I went."

The detective blinked a few times, almost like he was trying to contain a reaction. "Yes, well, that is her style."

I ignored the detective's remark and looked at Joey. "How did you happen to be looking right there at that moment?"

"It wasn't just at that moment. We watched Barbara and Walter strolling around—we saw them as soon as they got off their boat. It's not a wide channel, across the water, so we were all crouched down, waiting for them to move farther away—I'm sure you can guess people hang out down there for *privacy*, if you know what I mean. Discreet meetings don't welcome strolling couples."

My heart started to beat. "If you were so intent on

watching them, you must've seen at least a glimpse of the person who dropped the anchor."

He nodded. "Yeah, we weren't the only ones focused on them. The guy was leaned over, waiting for them. As they approached, the guy pulled out the anchor and dropped it. It happened so fast I didn't have time to warn her. If only I'd gone to see what that freak was doing, I could've stopped him—" A gurgle escaped his throat again and he buried his face into his mother's shoulder. Jane held him as he let it all out.

Her determined unwillingness to unmask any emotion was betrayed by a single tear that rolled down her cheek.

Detective Jones waited patiently to continue his questions. No doubt he realized allowing Joey to unburden himself of his pent up emotion would free him to think with a clearer mind.

I now heard sobbing coming from behind me. I looked around the room and saw Melanie folded up into her father's large frame. He leaned his head on hers and quietly tried to soothe her. Jane instructed her husband to take their daughter to her bedroom and fetch her a hot tea with a splash of whisky. He nodded and the pair left in silence.

Joey's blotchy face reappeared out of his mother's firm embrace. He looked ready for the inevitable questions he needed to face.

Detective Jones looked at Joey with raised eyebrows as if asking him if he was prepared to continue.

Joey took a deep breath and nodded, struggling to

look each of us in the eye. His mother kept him close.

The detective's pencil was poised as he cleared his throat. "Joey, what can you tell me about this person you saw watching Barbara and Walter Wiggins approach the underpass?"

"His face was covered by a cloth or hood or some-thing—I never got a good look. He seemed to be crouched down, like he was trying to hide, but still stick-ing out his neck to see them. I'm gonna find that neck—but I won't be hiding in the shadows. I want him to see what's coming."

Jane pulled her son back—he had begun to lean for-ward as his anger poured out. "Detective Jones, I'm sure you can understand my son's hurt and confusion over what has happened to my cousin. Of course, he means to do no harm—not even to someone who might deserve it. We respect the police and have full confidence that an arrest will be made quickly—especially now that you've heard a first-hand account of the violent attack."

The detective looked her in the eye. "We will do everything we can to find the killer. I'm sure I don't need to inform you, however, that it would've been helpful to hear Joey's account at the time of the incident."

"If he hadn't been threatened by that awful Bob Cole, I'm sure he would've been running to tell you, De-tective. Seems as if fate had its way with that man. We can only hope as much for the murderer himself."

A shiver ran down my back. "Jane, Detective Jones is an excellent police officer. I'm sure he'll solve the case."

She strained to make her face look pleasant. "Yes, as long as you are there to help him."

Detective Jones shot me a look as if I'd said the comment myself. Then he turned to her. "If it sets you at ease to involve Mrs. Walsh, I'd be happy for her to act as a liaison between us, if she's up for it. As you've stated, she has been helpful to us in the past."

I felt all eyes on me. I nodded automatically. It didn't seem like there was any other option.

"I have one last question," the detective said, as he stood up, his notebook still open, "Where were you when Barbara was killed?"

Joey looked confused. "I just told you—"

"I wasn't asking you, Joey," he turned to Jane. "I was asking your mom."

Jane's face went from pale to red almost instantly. "My husband and I were at the club, like we always are on Friday nights."

"Good to know. No need to walk me out. I'll be in touch."

With that he tipped his hat at each of us and left the house unceremoniously.

It was the first time, since the day I met Jane Humphries, that I was certain she liked someone else less than she liked me.

Chapter 25

I left the Humphries residence shortly after Detective Jones. The overflowing tap of emotion had drained the family of its ability to focus. They needed time to heal and regroup. I promised Jane I'd give her a call the next day with any updates I had. Tragedy could bring the best or the worst out in people. I never would have guessed that the person I'd liked least in town could've impressed me so much by the strength and compassion she showed her son.

Unfortunately, the revelation Joey bestowed upon us put a dark cloud over the already graying skies of Twin Oaks. There was no longer any doubt that Barbara's death was an accident. A murderer was in our midst.

It was time to catch a killer.

With the amount of facts and details unearthed at the Humphries, I felt as if I knew what an archaeologist might feel upon finding a large grouping of ancient relics or bones. The difference, of course, was I had hoped to learn more about Barbara Wiggins's very recent death.

But as more information came to light, there seemed more questions than answers.

Although Detective Jones hadn't given any details about how Bob Cole died, he let us know that it was suspicious. With the detective convinced the two deaths were related, I had no reason to doubt his assertion, which made it less important to know how he died—at least for now. The most important question I wanted answered was whether anyone else in our small town was at risk. I was anxious to talk to Detective Jones and find out his thoughts but I knew there was somewhere I had to go first.

Ava and I were both about as patient as a three-year-old waiting for dessert. Although I was worse in most cases, Ava couldn't be put off if there was something she needed or, more often, wanted. I knew as I approached her house that she was likely going out of her mind wondering where I had gone. No doubt she had already been to my house looking for me. Ava hated to be out of the loop.

I approached her home and found her sitting serenely in a chaise lounge on her front lawn. Of course, I knew not to trust the perfect picture of patience. Before I had my hand brake pulled, she had flung her sunglasses in the air and was marching purposefully toward my little car.

"Just what part of promise do you not understand?" Ava demanded.

"I'm sorry I wasn't home when you got back. How was the club?"

Her nose wrinkled in disgust. "Are you actually ask-

ing me about leisurely pastimes when our town has become embroiled in crime?"

I raised my eyebrows. "You have no idea."

Her feigned disgust was tossed away like her sunglasses and she hurried me to her front porch, where a
cozy swing-for-two hung. "I'm all ears."

She was true to her word and kept quiet. I updated
her, unraveling moment by moment, from the time she
left my house earlier this morning, to the second I pulled
into her driveway.

When I was finally done, I sat back and waited to
hear her thoughts. After a moment of silence, I realized I
had one more item to add to my long list of hard-to-
fathom moments from today. Ava Russell utterly
astounded, completely at a loss for words.

"More than you expected?" I asked.

She looked at me sideways. "The big slice of pie I
got with my coffee was more than I expected."

"Unfathomable?"

"Now that's more like it."

Ava could sometimes be melodramatic, but this time
her reaction seemed spot on. I had no doubt it would be
shared by most of Twin Oaks.

I considered the rippling effect of shock, and likely
fear, the news of back-to-back murders would spark. "I
certainly don't envy the pressure Detective Jones will be
under once all this becomes public."

She nodded. "People will demand answers—and
rightly so. Whoever is doing this must be brought to jus-
tice before someone else turns up dead. Any chance your

keen intuition is pointing at Joey as the likeliest killer? It sure would bring a fast and tidy end to all this."

I shook my head. "No, I really don't think so. He seemed genuinely broken up about the murder of Barbara, especially over having witnessed the whole thing. No, I think whoever did this was clever yet cool-headed."

"How do you figure?" she asked.

"Think about it—Joey hadn't planned on stashing that anchor in the bushes. He arrived early and got side-tracked by friends that he just happened to run into while waiting for Bob Cole. Whoever killed Barbara must've been watching nearby and took the opportunity to grab it and then use it to murder her."

Ava sat up and looked me in the eye. "So you think the killer was watching Barbara?"

"Yes, I do. She and Walter were on full display, sitting on the deck of their boat, having a splendid time, for all to see. Something about that must've enraged the killer—set him off enough to take the opportunity presented and kill her with no hesitation then slyly disappear into the night."

Ava looked at me in horror. "You're right. She was a sitting duck."

I nodded. "What I haven't figured out is how Bob Cole's death ties into it."

"Maybe it doesn't," Ava offered.

"It must," I argued. "There are too many ties between them. Think about it—Bob Cole just witnessed Barbara's murder. Then he's killed just yards away, a few days later? I refuse to believe there isn't a link somehow."

"That's not everything. You're keeping something from me."

I bit my lip. "You're right. Something is nagging me. I can't put my finger on it but I feel like there's a clue right in front of me that I just can't see—something important."

Ava shrugged. "Well, it seems like you've found yourself smack in the middle of another murder case. And considering the stakes, I don't think you should be left alone. If whoever did this was willing to kill two people—one possibly because they witnessed the first, then there's not a chance I'm letting you out of my sight until all this is cleared up."

"Don't you think that's a little over the top?"

"No, I don't. Everyone in town knows your reputation. If the killer gets even a hint that you are on his trail, you could be next on his list."

I pressed my lips together. "Perhaps that'll give me just the motivation I need to get my mind moving."

"Are you really sassing me right now?" Ava asked.

"It seemed like an opportune time."

"Stop talking and start thinking," she demanded.

"Yes, ma'am."

Ava left me on the swing. She went to get changed. It was Tuesday and we had to get to the club to meet Mary and Jo for our weekly lunch. I looked down at myself and wondered if there would be time to stop at my place, too. I turned to look at the reflection in the window overlooking the porch. My hair was tied up in a ponytail and I had a navy collared shirt paired with clam diggers.

It reminded me of Robin's outfit from the other day. While perhaps a little casual, I figured if a style maven could get away with it, so could I. Good thing, too, since it was almost noon. I hollered inside for Ava to hurry up and waited in the car. I decided then and there that I was done making plans for the rest of the afternoon. I was ready to go where fate wanted to take me. I just hoped I had the wherewithal to handle whatever was in store.

Chapter 26

It was busy at the club, which didn't surprise me one bit. From daybreak to sunset, Twin Oaks Country Club was a place built for lunching ladies and their hobnobbing hubbies. Just a few years earlier I desperately tried to avoid this place. However, the more time I spent there, the more I seemed to like it. My distaste for its exclusive and formal atmosphere had been tempered by my enjoyment of its incomparable facilities and grounds.

Tennis and golf were two of its most popular activities, but the beautiful gardens, expansive walking paths, and lovely social areas, complete with tiptop service, were the factors that broke my resolve and won me over. It would be easy to lose an entire day there, spending time with friends as I was pampered in the sun, without a care in the world. Ava had fallen for its charms too, and had become convinced that joining the club was an absolute must—for both of us.

I was quite happy when she informed me on our way

over that she was engineering a move to get us beyond the guest list and onto the full members list, complete with its members-only privileges and perks. According to Ava, it was no easy task to sign-up—one couldn't simply express an interest and expect an offer of welcoming. It took a member's nomination and the board's approval before a new addition would even be considered. Mary, who had been a member for several years, could sponsor us of course, but we would still be at the mercy of the board for final approval. I was on the verge of telling Ava to exclude me from the entire elitist process when we entered the gateway to the gardens and I saw the tulips in full bloom. My resolve was no match for the love I had for spring blooms in sunshine. All arguments against the distasteful process evaporated like morning dew on delicate pink petals. With a deep breath I inhaled the sweet smell of spring and a slow exhale swept away all righteous indignation.

It didn't take long before we found Mary, her bright scarf and warm smile easy to spot in a crowd. She was sitting at a round table with an open red umbrella that gave a generous amount of shade. Sipping what looked to be sparkling water with lime, Mary was a picture of relaxation—a feeling I envied after the intense morning I'd just had. She gave us a little wave, and we were happy to join her circle of calm. I felt someone touch my shoulder as I approached the table. It gave me a start and I whipped my head around to see Jo, looking apologetic at the reaction she caused in me.

I shook my head in embarrassment and gave our

youngest career-minded friend a hug. "Sorry, Jo, I guess I'm about as wound up as that twist in Mary's drink."

She grinned at me. "Should I order you a double?"

I gave her elbow a squeeze. "Only if it's caffeine. I'm a full-fledged teetotaler of late so I'll keep my indulgence to coffee."

Ava shushed me and put an arm around both of us. She then leaned in, to ensure her words wouldn't be overheard. "The prohibitionist over here is even insisting I abstain. I'm don't mind adhering to her un-wild ways, but I do have a reputation to uphold."

I fought an urge to laugh and pushed her off me. "If Mae West can do it sober, so can you, my friend."

"Good point," Ava conceded.

"Besides," I added, "I don't recall ever actually insisting on anything like that."

Ava threw her arms up in the air. "Kindred spirits and all that. I can't indulge and allow you to see I'm full of nonsense. It would completely put us out of sync. Besides, my waist actually shrank an inch in the process. So, you'll hear no complaints from me."

My mouth shot open as we each took a seat. "You never mentioned that to me before. Why didn't my waist do that? Now I suddenly have the urge to complain."

A waiter came over and brought some menus for us to peruse. Ava ordered some deviled eggs to start, raising one eyebrow provocatively at me as she did so. I rolled my eyes and bit my lip to stop myself from laughing out loud.

Mary watched our exchange and took off her sunglasses to take a better look at us. "What has gotten into to you two today?"

Jo put her hand over Mary's. "If it's what I think, they are just letting off some steam. There've been some awful happenings around here. I'd better fill you in."

Since Jo began working at the newspaper, she naturally monitored the heart of our town. Because she was at the most current source for breaking news, she kept us well informed as she learned the happenings around town.

Although still working mostly behind the scenes, with an occasional human-interest piece, the newspaper staff was small and tight-knit, so there were few secrets in her office. I was relieved not to have to repeat the news of the day, feeling the laughter leave my body as we began to discuss the reality and severity of recent events.

Mary echoed the same thoughts Ava and I had shared earlier in the day—shock and concern were communally felt. While we all knew Barbara Wiggins, I wondered how well Mary knew Bob Cole. Ava and I, like most of the home-owners in town, knew him from dealings with our mortgages, at the very least. Mary owed nothing to anyone. She was in a class of wealth beyond even the richest in our affluent small town. Her father, against all tradition, ensured she was educated in school and money. She was left the majority of the family wealth when he passed, and he made sure she would never give up control of it to anyone, including her husband. As it turned out, her dad was right to do so—

Mary's husband was a terrible man, whose own demons led to his early demise.

Before I could even ask the question, Ava brought it up in a roundabout way. "Mary," she began, "I know this is off-topic, but I wondered if you'd heard anything about our applications to the club. Izzy and I need something to help us feel better in these dismal times."

Mary smiled. "It's funny you should ask. Just the other day, I attended a board meeting and inquired about just that. Apparently, there has been a number of people interested in joining, not the least of which, of course, is you two, *and* the late Mr. Cole."

I sat up. "Bob Cole wanted to become a member? Why?"

Ava seemed just as surprised, mimicking my movements. "That man hated everybody."

Mary sighed. "I don't think it was his idea."

I was confused. "Whose idea was it? Last I heard, he and the Mrs. rarely socialized together."

"Yes," Mary nodded. "Well, it seems it was more of a business decision—and not his own. You see, the owners of Twin Oaks Bank, the same owners who run a few other banks from a few neighboring towns, seemed to have decided that the crème-de-la-crème of its organization—the executives, should become members of the club."

"Why?" Jo asked.

Mary frowned. "So they could use our club to entertain prospective clients in a suitable atmosphere."

Ava raised her eyebrows. "Is that allowed?"

"Not exactly," Mary explained. "But the board said they would consider each applicant on a case-by-case, person-by-person, basis. Nine out of ten of the candidates were approved."

Ava scoffed. "Geez, that sounds rather humiliating."

I wondered. "What was considered unacceptable about the one person? Was it financial?"

Mary shook her head. "Not at all. The bank offered to pay all memberships and fees of each of their employees. It's a big cash influx for the club, which is very attractive this year in particular, since we are considering a huge undertaking—an Olympic-sized outdoor pool."

"That would cost a fortune," I commented.

"Exactly. That's why it was almost universally approved. Except for that one."

Jo looked at her suspiciously. "Why do I get the feeling you're holding something back?"

Mary looked around to make sure no one else was in earshot. "The person snubbed made it very clear he was displeased by the decision—stormed in here a few weeks ago and caused a very rare scene. The timing of it all just seems very odd. You see girls, the person in question was Bob Cole."

Jo slammed down her hands. "What a coincidence!"

Her utterance reminded me of something Detective Jones had said just the other day. *Coincidences of this sort are rare.*

Ava must've seen my expression darken. "Uh-oh. What is it, Izzy?"

I looked at her. "Joey said something this morning. I

can't help wonder whether it's connected somehow," I paused and looked at Mary. "What did Bob Cole say when he caused a scene? Any chance he cast blame for his humiliating rejection on a certain board member?"

Mary looked surprised. "Why, yes, he did. And to be honest, he was right on the money. Most of us, you see, were focused more on the influx of cash instead of the character of the ten applicants. We were ready to sweep them all in, and begin plans for development. But one member absolutely refused on his account. She just wouldn't budge. We gave in to her will and told the bank. They accepted our decision without argument," Mary frowned and looked at me. "I don't know how he found out. Our meetings are confidential. But besides all that, how did you know, Izzy?"

I didn't answer, instead pressing on as my thoughts unravelled. "I'm not sure yet, but I get the feeling it's important. Mary, was Jane Humphries the board member who refused to give in?"

No one answered. My three friends had shifted their attention to directly behind me instead. I turned around slowly and looked at a perfectly polished version of the woman in question. She was standing directly over me, looking down. She responded to my sheepish smile with a ferocious grin. "Did I hear someone say my name?"

I could feel goose bumps crawl up my arms and I instinctively tried to rub them away. "Jane, hello. I was just mentioning to my friends that we ran into each other earlier."

She looked up and nodded to Mary, Ava, and Jo.

"Yes, of course. Speaking of that, might I have a word, Isabelle?"

I nodded and got up, following her lead, away from my friends. I looked back at them and hoped I would live to see them another day. Ava seemed to be trying to give me last minute coaching advice, putting her dukes up and swinging subtly. I stifled a laugh then prayed Jane didn't overhear my flippant overture.

She led me to a private setting just behind some trees, away from listening ears. "I'd like to talk to you about what you heard at my home, earlier today."

"Of course. Is Joey okay?" I asked.

"He will be, with our help. That's why I'm here, Isabelle. I need your help."

I looked at her with surprise. "When Melanie told you she had asked for my help you seemed wary about the idea."

"That's before I knew all the facts, or at least, the facts so far. I'm not a people pleaser the way you and your friends are. But I will do anything to help my family—it's too late for my cousin but not for my son. And at this point he needs all the help he can get."

I couldn't argue with that.

"I watched you with Joey. You were kind to him and you believe in him, I can see that. Please, Isabelle, I'm asking you mother-to-mother. Please help my son."

"Jane, I will help him any way I can but I know Detective Jones well enough to see he believed what Joey was saying. I don't think Joey is a suspect anymore."

"Maybe not. But Joey is in trouble. Whoever killed

my cousin and Bob Cole has him in their sights."

"Jane, we don't even know whether the two murders are connected."

"Izzy, please. They may not be on paper, but can you tell me you don't think they're related?"

"No, I can't argue with you there."

"And Joey?" she demanded.

"If it were my son, I'd be worried, too. Okay, Jane. I see your point. I'll do whatever I can to help. But I'm going to need your help in return."

"What do you mean?"

"I have a few conditions."

She seemed to stiffen at my words.

"First," I continued, "I need you to agree to include my friends. Mary has a wide network of friends who seem to know stuff, Jo has an inside scoop and resources at the newspaper, and Ava…"

She groaned at her name.

"And Ava," I repeated, "Because she is my partner-in-crime."

"Interesting choice of words," she complained.

"The second thing—"

"There's more?"

"Yup. The second thing is that you are completely open with me about what you know and what you don't. Whoever killed your cousin and Bob Cole is at an advantage. He knows us but we don't know him. Detective Jones is an excellent police officer, but we know this town and its people—and something tells me that gives us an insight that he doesn't have. So, what do you think?"

"I think I should get out an old hat box and put away my pride." When I didn't respond, she lightly grabbed my elbow then looked me in the eye. "That was a joke. I am thankful for your willingness to help my family. I hope you know I mean that."

I nodded. "Now, let's go talk to the rest of our team. There's a lot we need to discuss. But—" I paused. "Maybe leave the joke-telling to Lucille Ball."

We walked back to where my friends sat and I invited Jane to sit down. I could feel the razor sharp focus Ava set upon me. I was breaking the cardinal rule of inviting an enemy into our sacred circle. I wondered if Ava would soften if I reminded her of an episode of *I Love Lucy* from last year where Lucy befriended a band known as "friends of the friendless." I supposed I could argue it was our turn. I smiled at the thought then caught Ava's fiery gaze. *No.* She was in no mood for humor, either. I sighed. It was going to be a long afternoon.

Chapter 27

It felt like a long session of Q&A instead of our weekly lunch date, but the hours spent consolidating what each of us knew was well worth the sacrifice. It was nearing dinnertime by the time our party broke up. Ava was already past when she should've been home and I was glad to have the excuse to leave. On our way out to the parking lot, we walked past a lively room, full of men smoking cigars and drinking spirits. It seemed odd to have such a lively tone before the dinner hour. I spotted a few familiar faces among the crowd, including Grant Marshall, the handsome bank executive, who was actually standing on a chair, looking like he was about to deliver a speech. I caught his eye as we passed, and he tipped his glass at me with a grin. I returned his smile, wondering if there was any way it might be some sort of remembrance for Bob Cole. I thought of the misery the dead bank manager generously doled out in his life and dismissed the thought, having a brief moment of guilt at my own harshness.

It made me consider how much my opinion of Jane Humphries had changed virtually overnight. Curious as always, I asked Ava her thoughts on Jane as soon as we were on the road, out of earshot of the club.

Ava seemed to consider the question carefully before answering. "Can I just say that she surprised me?"

I shook my head. "Nope. You gave me the look of death when I brought her over. Now I must insist you have a slice of humble pie."

She wrinkled her nose. "I've never been a fan. As a best friend, can you not let me off the hook?"

"As a *best friend,*" I emphasized, "I will help you maintain an air of modesty. Now go on, say it. She was pleasant."

"She was tolerable."

I lowered my sunglasses and gave her my most motherly expression.

She slapped her knee and pretended to take a bite of the fresh ocean breeze. "Fine. She was perfectly pleasant. Although sometimes displaying a sour expression, she was never anything other than considerate and helpful. In other words, completely unlike her usual self. You happy now?"

I smiled and nodded.

"Good. Now, can I request a little warning next time you decide to befriend a sworn enemy?"

"Fair enough," I said as I pulled into her driveway. "You in for the night?"

She nodded reluctantly. "I promised Bruce I'd even attempt an orange chiffon cake with buttercream icing if I put him and the kids through another dinner of poached eggs and canned ham. Judging by the time, I better dust off the old hand mixer."

"Don't you mean get it out of the unopened box?"

"Yes, which will also require a little dusting. I left it out prominently after Christmas last year. Bruce thought it was because I intended to use it—it took a while but after making sure the duster missed it each and every time, he got the hint to never waste his money on baking gadgets again."

"You're a clever lady."

"True. Which means I know you are planning on a little twilight fishing—and not at George's creek."

I couldn't argue.

"Just make sure you find someone to back you up. Perhaps it's time to even request a little help from a real detective?"

"I was just thinking—"

She put up her hand. "Yes, that's how it always begins."

"I was going to say that I was just thinking I'd stop by the police department tomorrow morning to see if Detective Jones was around."

She looked at me with one eyebrow raised. "How sensible of you. Now, go directly home and make sure to call me when you arrive. Let me know you're okay."

"Yes, boss."

We bid good-bye and I drove away. My thoughts immediately returned to the enlightening conversation from earlier that day. What had we learned? To begin with, we confirmed what we already suspected—that Barbara was losing interest in her business. But Jane scoffed at the notion that it stemmed from marital pressures. According to her, Barbara had already lost interest in the shop and was exaggerating the pressure Walter had applied because she didn't want to seem fickle. When I reminded Jane of Walter's temper tantrum the day Barbara was killed, Jane blamed his display more on the immediate humiliation he suffered at the hands of the bank than anything else. The blatant link to Bob Cole was undeniable, unfortunately, Jane had no further insight into the connection between the two murders than what we already knew.

However, she did enlighten us on her son's recent activities. It seemed Joey's recent brush with the law was not exactly out-of-nowhere. When asked about her son's recent troubles, she hesitated and then, with a seldom-seen slump in the shoulders paired with a deep sigh, she seemed to resign herself to the fact that she was going to trust us, like it or not.

She told us Joey had recently begun to sneak out of the house at night. A few weeks before the murder, a noise woke her. She initially thought it was a burglar climbing up the trellis, but found out, as she peeked out her bedroom window, it was actually Joey doing just the opposite. Her controlling nature—she called it motherly concern—squashed her initial urge to stop him—demanding instead that she find out exactly where her son was intending to go. She woke her husband up and asked him to follow Joey but he refused, saying their son

was probably just out meeting a girl. By the time she realized it was up to her, Joey had already disappeared into
the night. She waited up for him in silent darkness, ensuring he wouldn't find out she was onto him. Fraught with
worry, she promised herself she wouldn't make the same
mistake the next time. The following morning, she put
together an outfit, appropriate for comfort and camou-
flage, and tucked it under her bed. Her normal tendency
to sleep lightly naturally amplified and she knew his next
night out would not go undetected. Less than a week later, Joey repeated his sneaky behavior and Jane was
ready. Dressed in seconds, Jane stealthily followed him,
determined to find out what he was up to and with whom.
She stayed well-hidden and far enough back—he never
suspected a thing. Much to Jane's disappointment, Joey
went straight to Cooper's Bridge, descending into the
darkness, where she knew he would be doing nothing to
talk about in church. Jane didn't follow any closer,
choosing instead to hunker down and wait. At that point,
she was not ready to jeopardize her secret presence. After
almost an hour he emerged, cigarette in hand, with a
swagger in his step she immediately recognized as one
brought on by an excess of alcohol. Fury contained, she
followed him home and watched him climb back into his
upstairs window, once again.

The third time she followed him, she waited until he
was on his way back home and crept quietly down to see
who and what was attracting her impressionable young
son. It was no surprise to see a small group of young
men, obviously led by one older boy, who the rest

seemed to pander to. They were all partaking in drinking, smoking, and a lot of posturing.

The pattern repeated with her beginning to take notes on who was there and what took place. She knew most of the faces and made it her mission to find out the names and identities of those she did not. In particular, she wanted to know who the dominant male was, in charge of leading these impressionable young men down a path of corruption. He seemed to be providing the goods by which the younger men were getting drunk and disorderly.

Jane guessed these sinful, unchecked behaviors would likely escalate, and she was right. They didn't stay confined to the bridge for long. The oldest boy was leading them into the streets. He was directing and daring the willing young men to cause mischief. Spray paint, vandalism, and destruction began to take over their time out. Joey partook, albeit without the vigour shown by some— according to Jane.

Worried about her son getting into trouble with the law, Jane decided not to enlist the help of the police. Instead, she took matters into her own hands. With Joe, Sr.'s old service revolver tucked into her side, she waited for Joey to depart his delinquent friends at the end of a long night of causing mischief, then went under the bridge, where the evenings always seemed to start and end. I was not surprised to hear the head troublemaker was, like so many others, no match for Jane. The domineering protective mother descended into the forefront of the group quickly and turned the gun on the one she believed to be the leader of the loosely organized gang. She told him if he ever enlisted her son to do his dirty work again, he'd regret it. Excessively cooperative with her, the young hooligan identified himself as Arnold Riley and swore never to associate himself with her son again.

She accepted his declaration but decided to ensure he'd keep it by demanding to know where he lived and then visiting his home, where she banged on the door. Her strong belief in parental involvement and control made it necessary to inform Arnold's mother and father about their delinquent son's recent decision to recruit other young men into trouble. Much to Jane's surprise, they did not thank her for her good deed nor take kindly to her description of their only son, stating he was just letting off steam, frustrated by the strict rules placed on him by people like her.

Subsequently, they stated their son would not have the means to purchase all the sinful indulgences she observed, suggesting Joey, in fact, was more likely to have provided the funding necessary to acquire the so-called corruptive substances. Offended and confused by their obvious lack of morality and sense, she left, convinced the entire family was a lost cause.

In spite of her last meeting, Jane assumed all involved heeded her warnings and obeyed her commands. She went back to a regular sleep pattern, having thought it had all been sorted out. It was not until Joey's arrest, the morning after Barbara was murdered, she realized perhaps Joey *had* brought on some of his own troubles, having no one left to blame. Joey must've snuck out undetected, continuing on his troubled path, and finally landing square in the clutches of Bob Cole. With his moral compass compromised, he likely felt completely incapable of resisting the threats against him from the evil, conniving, and powerful man.

When I pulled into my driveway, a few minutes later, I was still churning things over in my head. I began to piece together the timeline of events involving the mother and son's clandestine movements compared to when the two murders took place. The overlap of time and location were striking. That is not to say I believed Joey or his audacious mother were directly involved in the deaths of either Barbara or Mr. Cole, but somehow, I was now convinced there must be a link.

I thought back to when I foolishly tried to check out the underbelly of the bridge a few days earlier. By Jane's description, I would guess the intimidating young man who greeted me was likely the same leader of the gang Jane challenged. I wondered if Detective Jones had gained any insight into him or the group that might raise any red flags.

Then there was Mr. Cole and the botched theft of the anchor-turned-murder weapon. What was his initial motivation? When and why had he become desperate enough to consider breaking the law to achieve some unbeknownst end goal?

There was a note tucked into the doorway from Detective Jones. He wanted me to go by the station at my earliest convenience, underlining there was no imminent urgency. After popping inside to powder my nose and have a glass of water, I headed back out, focused on the task ahead. Perhaps that was why I didn't notice the tall, obscure figure lurking in the nearby bushes, in the shadows of the sinking sun.

Chapter 28

Detective Jones looked tired. He was slouched over his desk, tapping a pencil on some papers he was looking at. When the desk charge greeted me with a friendly hello, it prompted the detective to look up. His drawn face seemed to brighten a little. He called over to the junior officer, instructing him to let me in, which the young man did. I approached the detective and, with a nod of his head, he led me toward the back of the station, out of public view, where there were private rooms. He paused to offer me a coffee, which I accepted automatically, hoping he might have a stash of treats hidden somewhere nearby. He opened an adjacent drawer, as if reading my mind, and grabbed a box of sugar wafers.

We carried on, down the hall, and stopped at a doorway. He entered and I followed. There was a small plain table with a chair on each side. One chair was cushioned and comfortable-looking and the other was basic and wooden. I automatically took the wooden chair, well aware it was normally where a suspect would sit when they were being interviewed by an investigator. Detective Jones did not argue.

He paused to select a cookie and enjoy a sip of coffee. Then he sat across for me and leaned back in his chair. "I'm not used to having to seek you out these last few days, Mrs. Walsh."

"I suppose that's true. But don't worry, I've been keeping busy," I said.

"Oh, really?"

I wasn't sure if he was asking or commenting. I was unfazed. "I've been at the club most of the day with friends. I came here as soon as I saw your note."

He leaned forward on the desk and clasped his hands together. "With two unsolved murders under your nose, I can't see you spending the day filling your social calendar. Mind telling me what you were up to?"

When did he get to know me so well?

I paused and considered my answer carefully. "I was having lunch with my friends."

He drew back. "Mm-hm. Normally, that would sound perfectly innocent. But I know your friends."

I swallowed. "I suppose you do. Although it was more than just the regular posse, as you've referred to us in the past—Ava, Mary, Jo, and me. Jane Humphries joined us and the lunch extended beyond its regular timeslot."

"Any reason?"

I wasn't sure if he wanted to know if there was a reason behind the visit from Jane or the lingering lunch. "Well, there are a few things I found out," I paused. "Any chance to keep this meeting out of your notebook and a little less official?"

He seemed to consider the question. Then he stood up. "It's a nice evening. Up for a stroll?"

I happily complied, recognizing this as his way of giving me the opportunity to talk to him more informally, without documenting what I said or involuntarily sharing information with curious nearby ears. It was also a great opportunity to get a glimpse of the setting sun and the glorious array of colors framing it—a much nicer setting for a conversation, even if the topic was murder.

The police station was fairly close to the town square. We chose it as our goal and walked along the well-maintained pedestrian boulevard for a few minutes in silence, before returning to where the conversation had left off.

When the detective asked again about my lunch at the club, I filled him in on our conversation with Jane Humphries, explaining the details regarding Joey and his troublesome activities with the so-called gang. Detective Jones listened carefully and didn't seem at all surprised by what I told him. He made no comment, but I guessed that since he kept surveillance on the group—which was almost jeopardized by my careless wandering the other day—Detective Jones was well aware of the types of activities they partook in. I was relieved he wasn't in the mood to ask any more details regarding Joey, whom, I guessed, had now been crossed off the suspect list.

When the topic of what I knew seemed exhausted, I hoped he might share any insight he might have with me.

"Detective Jones, might I inquire as to why you summoned me this evening?"

He looked at me amusedly before answering. "I didn't realize I held that much power."

I blushed. "You know what I mean."

He nodded. "Of course. I conducted an interview earlier today. Your name was brought up and it left me feeling uneasy. It seemed like a good idea to fill you in."

I wasn't expecting to be the subject of discussion. "I'm listening."

"Good. However, before we get into all that, I need you to be caught up with a few interesting facts—namely, that I got a tip about the anchor used to kill Barbara Wiggins. I followed up and got confirmation that it had very recently been insured for a considerable amount of money."

"Does that come as a surprise?"

"Not once I found out its value—it hadn't occurred to me that an anchor could be worth so much."

I was curious. "Is that because of its uniqueness? A collector's item?"

"No, it's more basic than that—the anchor is solid gold."

My eyebrows shot up. "That must be worth a fortune."

"At just over thirty-five dollars an ounce, that twenty-five-pound anchor could net a tidy sum. A discreet goldsmith could help the thief pocket over fourteen thousand dollars."

"That's a lot of money. But hasn't it been sitting at

the museum for years? Why would someone steal it now?"

"That a good question, Mrs. Walsh. And, as you know, I'm a big believer in timing. I wondered the same thing—so I was quite intrigued when I learned through Bob Cole's recent files that it was *he* who insured the anchor very recently."

I looked at him. "Oh, my goodness."

"That's not all. The museum was out-of-date and the new curator was attempting to get things in order. Part of that was documenting everything they held and protecting precious and valuable items through the bank. There were less than ten items insured, and the anchor was, by far, the most valuable of the lot."

"I see." My mind started turning. "If Mr. Cole felt his position at the bank was threatened, which it seems he did, I could see how access to a windfall of cash might be tempting. My guess is he, like most of the town, would have had no idea the museum housed such a valuable piece."

The detective nodded. "I agree."

His words encouraged me to continue. "Recognizing Joey unexpectedly—knowing his relation to Barbara—the person he likely blamed for his tarnished career, might have given him the idea to use the vulnerable young man to steal it."

"Do you think so?"

I nodded adamantly. "Absolutely. There would be minimal risk. The truth is, if Joey got caught, Mr. Cole would deny any involvement and Joey would take all the blame."

The detective studied me closely. "That makes a lot of sense. Now, my question for you—do you think Mr. Cole would've recognized Joey? Known his family connection to Mrs. Wiggins?"

I had no doubt. "There's something every resident of Twin Oaks knew about Bob Cole. The man ran the bank as if he owned every penny within its walls. If you had any dealings there, he knew who you were, what you owned, and what you owed. No one escaped notice. Asking for a loan, a mortgage, or any other major financial transaction was strictly through him."

"Thank you. That clarifies things."

"Does that mean Joey is still a suspect?"

He considered the question. "It probably should but after our talk today, I don't see him having the gumption for it."

"And Darryl Walker?"

"Your old classmate seems to have a lot of knowledge and experience," he said.

I tapped my bottom lip. "Is he the new curator at the museum?"

"Yes, as of a few months back."

"I guess I had assumed he worked there in a more basic position. Does that mean his name was on the insurance papers?"

"Yes, right next to Bob Cole's."

That wasn't good.

"So how did my name get brought up?" I asked.

"Mr. Walker seemed convinced you tipped me off."

I frowned. "Tipped you off about what?"

Detective Jones sighed. "High school."

I scrunched my nose. "I'm guessing he didn't think take kindly to that."

He stopped and turned to look me in the eye. "No, he didn't."

"I can see why he would be upset. High school was a long time ago and he was treated unfairly—by everyone. I almost didn't mention the trouble between he and Barbara because I knew it would make him a suspect. I feel a little guilty."

"How would you feel if it turned out that we had a murderer on the loose because you were afraid of telling me what you knew?"

"You think he killed Barbara and Mr. Cole?"

He shook his head. "That's not what I said."

"But it is what you implied," I argued.

"Maybe, but I did it more for effect. Sometimes I forget you're always two steps ahead. My point is that the friendship you and I have built is based on trust."

"I appreciate that. But I doubt Darryl Walker does—more likely he sees me as a lonely widow desperately trying to make herself relevant using any means she can."

The detective gave me a sideways look. "I doubt it—you don't quite fit the profile."

My eyes widened in surprise.

He cleared his throat. "It's important that you are aware that Darryl sees what you did as a betrayal. I wouldn't expect a warm reception next time you see him. He harbors resentment about the past—and it's fast-forwarding to the present. I'd like you to stay clear of the museum for a while and keep your guard up."

If Darryl could become angry with me for simply re-telling history, I couldn't imagine the heightened emotion incited by an unexpected run-in with Barbara, the perpe-trator of his fall from the graces of Twin Oaks High.

Chapter 29

Barbara's funeral was set for Thursday morning. It would be held at the Smith-Crawley Funeral Home, the only funeral parlor in town, and there was little doubt it would be a big, busy affair. Ava asked me to accompany her shopping to pick out an appropriate outfit and I was happy to go along, ready for a break from thinking about the reason it was needed in the first place. I was beginning to worry that two murders, committed in cold blood, were going to go unsolved and unpunished. I hoped a few hours of shopping with Ava would distract me from my heavy woes.

My mood lightened at the sight of her, looking bright and chipper in a yellow gingham pencil dress. She cinched it in the middle with a slim belt and wore white gloves in which she carried a small black clutch. Since she was already at the curb, I barely slowed down before she hopped in and we were off. She peeked down at my simple red swing dress and seemed to approve. I knew she liked it when I wore bright colors, so I'd figured I'd oblige. I'd even matched my lipstick to it and flashed her a grin as I sped off en route to a day of fun.

Since I had no idea where we were going, I decided to slow down when we came to the top of the rocky hill just off Ava's street. She suggested we head down to Main Street.

I was ready to go for a cruise but she had other ideas—pointing to a parking spot, right in front of the now defunct Robin's Closet.

I gave Ava a questioning look. "You remember the store is closed, right?"

She crossed her arms and looked at me suspiciously. "Izzy, do you trust me?"

I raised an eyebrow. "Is that a trick question?"

She ignored my cheeky response and exited the car. I wasn't sure what she was up to but followed her anyways. As I suspected she went straight to the front door of the shop and knocked. I didn't ask any more questions but waited to see what my secretive friend was up to. It wasn't long before the lock was turned and the door swung open. Melanie Humphries looked surprised by our visit and welcomed us inside, where she and Robin Manners were clearly busy, organizing the last remnants of the boutique's stock.

Ava stepped up and gave each of the women a warm embrace. I smiled and waved behind her, throwing my hands up to let them know I had no idea what we were doing here either. Ava opened up her purse and took out two small gift-wrapped boxes.

She gave one to each of the women. "Jane mentioned at lunch yesterday you two would be here getting things wrapped up so Walter could finalize details before funeral tomorrow. I wanted to give each of you a small token of my gratitude for your excellent service and guidance for all things fashion."

"Ava, no wonder why you were always our favorite patron," Robin stated as she unwrapped the gift.

Melanie seconded Robin's sentiments. "This is beyond thoughtful."

Inside each box was a small bottle of Guerlain Shalimar perfume. "Exquisite," Robin said.

Melanie just squealed and clapped. "I love this stuff, it's divine."

Ava looked pleased. "It was also Barbara's favorite—at least it was years ago. I thought Barbara would appreciate it if we all wore it to the funeral as a way to honor her memory. I got one for you, too, Izzy. But it's at home. I couldn't fit them all in my purse."

I was touched. "When you do things like this, your reputation is jeopardized, you big softy."

She grinned. "This stays between us. Besides, I needed a good excuse to interrupt these two worker bees. We are in dire need of some good advice to find a nice boutique. When I woke up today, I realized I've been coming here for so long, I wasn't really sure where to go."

Robin nodded confidently as she dabbed a little perfume on her wrist. "If you're up for a drive I can give you the name of a shop I've been known to frequent in the city."

"Izzy, what say you?" Ava asked.

I nodded. "What's the point of having a fast car if you can't take it on the new freeway from time to time?"

"Great!" Ava exclaimed.

We got the address and directions and bid the ladies good-day with the unspoken knowledge the next time we'd be seeing each other was to bury Barbara, the following afternoon. I was glad to be doing something that would take my mind off the funeral. Since Frank's service, I had had a hard time not revisiting that day in my memory any time I was near Twin Oaks cemetery. I looked at myself in the rearview mirror as I tied my scarf around my hair and put on my stylish sunglasses. *You can do this.* I looked at Ava and felt strengthened by her supportive presence.

She looked back at me and flinched. "What are you smiling at?" she demanded, leaning over to look at herself in the sideview mirror. She bared her front teeth like a donkey soaking in the scent of a tasty ginger biscuit. "Do I have lipstick on my teeth?"

I emulated her raised lip and awkward grin. "I'm just happy to see you."

"You're an odd duck."

"No, I'm a smiling ass."

"You'll hear no argument from me."

Feeling better, I revved the engine and sped away from the curb. Sometimes there was just no other cure for a sad heart than a best friend.

We easily found the boutique recommended by Robin. Off Fifth Avenue, it was located just down the street from Grand Central Station. I could tell Ava was pleased from the moment we walked in, her eyes darting around from rack to rack, looking in admiration at all the styles housed within the small shop. There was only one sales woman there when we arrived and she and Ava hit it off almost as soon as we entered the doors. Ava gushed a little, and the woman seemed pleased by her admiration. I avoided the conversation initially, preferring to just wander on my own. But it wasn't long before Ava called me over, stating that I wouldn't believe what she just found out.

"Hi," I said to the saleslady, "I'm Isabelle."

The woman's name was Karen. Ava didn't seem to have time for our introduction, however, waving her hands to let me know she had something pressing to tell me. I focused back on her. "Ava, what did you find out?"

"Karen here knows Robin's Closet. I just told her about Barbara."

The woman nodded and looked at me. "I'm sorry to hear the shocking news. I've been to the shop before. My husband took me to Twin Oaks for brunch one day. It was lovely—both the town and the shop."

"Did you meet Barbara?" I asked.

"No, but I did meet Robin. I remember because of the shop's name matched hers. I told her if she ever wanted to relocate to Manhattan, I'd make it worth her while. She seemed intent to stay put, unfortunately. I've seen her a few times since, but it was here and I was always with another customer. I'm sorry to hear the store is closing and even more sorry to learn the reason for it."

Our conversation moved on to the clothing in stock. Ava wanted to get something appropriate for the funeral but fashionable enough to wear under cheerier circumstances. "Barbara would approve," Ava assured me as she ogled a wide-collared fitted black wool suit with subtle flecks of gold.

"It would look nice with pearls," I had to agree.

We left the shop feeling good. I picked up a simple but elegant black pencil skirt and white blouse, and Ava with the aforementioned suit. Both relieved, we were prepared for the next day's solemn event, we walked back to the car and talked about the logistics of it. We agreed that she and Bruce would pick me up just after ten and we would head over together. I was relieved to not have to go alone and she was intuitive enough to know it. I would call Mary and Jo to make sure we all coordinated a place in the funeral home together. Barbara may not have been well-liked, but she was well-known and respected, at least around the club. It would be a busy event. It would also be one I intended to watch carefully. With the murderer still unknown, I'd be looking out for subtle clues of any sort that might tip me off. I guessed Detective Jones would be there with the same intent.

After dropping off Ava, I went home and spent the rest of the day in my garden. I wished I could speed up the time and be two days ahead. That would give me the opportunity to see my kids and miss the funeral, all at once. Of course, it would also bring me much closer to my own business' quarterly meeting—scheduled for next week. After my visit to the bank the other day, I felt the urge to gain a better understanding of the business Frank left me—at least enough to follow any discussion that might come up. Bruce kept copies of everything and gave me one after every meeting. After clearing my garden of all prickly weeds starting to crop up, I figured I might as well get on it. I quickly set my hair for the next day then dusted off the top of the filing cabinet where the papers sat. I thought of the irony of the situation. I was finally doing a task I had put off for years in order to avoid thinking about the funeral of a woman who avoided the same task until her death.

I grabbed a bunch of documents and brought them to the sofa. I began to scan the first one. Within seconds, my head began to bob, my eyes began to droop, and I supposed Barbara and I had more in common that I realized—neither one of us seemed to have a penchant for business. It wasn't long before my weariness won, and I was dreaming of adding machines chasing me across the moon.

Chapter 30

Ava and Bruce picked me up at promptly at ten the next morning. It was not the sort of event to be fashionably late. We were meeting Jo and Mary at ten-thirty near the funeral home. I got ready early. My pink rubber curlers woke me just after dawn with pokes and pulls. Sleep was no longer an option—I was ready to get them out. I cursed myself for not taking the proper time to put them in, and seemed to learn the lesson each time I rushed the job. If they were not put in the proper spots as per instructions, they could be very uncomfortable to sleep in. I promised myself I would not be hasty again—for the sake of my delicate ears and tender scalp. Spoolies promised the possibility of a comfortable sleep and I was determined to prove it—next time.

At least getting up early gave me the opportunity to do a careful job on the setting and my makeup. By the time the sun rose, I felt perfectly presentable. Now, as long as I was able to stay awake, I should be in good form at the service. By the time my ride came by, I had

had three cups of coffee, breakfast, and a snack. I was so bored; I even began to look over the business documents I had brought out the night before. Even with no distractions, I had a hard time concentrating. I gave up and just flipped through the papers instead. Nothing stood out except the basic numbers on the financial statement—money going in and money going out. The bottom line showed a nice profit. At least I knew that much. It was so clearly displayed; it would have been impossible to miss. It convinced me that Barbara must've been aware of her numbers, too.

When Ava and Bruce picked me up, accounting was still on my mind. It was good timing, too, since Bruce was the star accountant who kept my books balanced as well as so many others. Since it was so rare that I was focused on numbers, I figured I had better take advantage of that focus before it slipped away.

"Bruce, what are your thoughts on Barbara's failed business?"

Ava looked at me with wide eyes but said nothing.

Bruce, too, looked a little surprised. "I'm not sure what could be said, Izzy. Businesses fail every day."

"Have you heard of businesses being sabotaged?" I asked.

"I suppose, but under what circumstance? From what I've been told, Barbara seemed to have lost interest in it. When bills aren't paid, and suppliers are stiffed, for example, it's normally a sign of mismanagement. Ava told me the store was busy, but it's not just as simple as that. One must keep on top of the numbers, if not the owner, someone designated to do so—like me, for you."

I nodded. "Yes, for which I am forever indebted."

"Frank was my friend. It's a privilege to oversee the business' success. Every business requires maintenance—even ones making money."

"But what if the person in charge wanted the business to fail?" I persisted.

Bruce took his glasses off and rubbed his eyes. He looked at me before putting them back on. "Ava recounted what Barbara inferred regarding getting back at her husband—for whatever reason—by causing the business to fail. But it sounds like an awful lot of effort to me. If Barbara wasn't interested anymore, wouldn't it just be easier to sell it and start a new hobby, if that's what it was to her?"

Ava held up her hand. "Barbara was never lazy in her pursuits. If her goal was to humiliate her husband, she would put in whatever effort was required to do so."

Bruce sighed. "I know you've said as much, but from a practical point-of-view, the numbers would take serious manipulation to do so. I mean, she didn't have the business that long. I don't know Walter Wiggins all that well, but I've never counted him as a fool. I would assume he would have had the business checked out thoroughly before buying it for his wife to take over. If I was Walter and had gone to that much trouble—put my reputation on the line to open up a business for my bored wife, only to find out she destroyed it on purpose, causing me extraordinary humiliation and financial strain, I can't even imagine how I'd react. I'd want to wring her neck."

Ava gently stroked her lithe, long neck as we talked. "Excuse me folks, your conversation is causing me some strain of my own. Besides, Walter was with Barbara when she died. Izzy, you watched him carry her body into the restaurant and Joey Humphries confirmed it, remember?"

"Yes, but a few things have been nagging me. First of all, I have to tell you I find it hard to believe that Walter gave Barbara carte blanche to run the business as she saw fit—especially when she was barely there. Would he really have had no checks and balances in place to make sure she wasn't doing exactly what she did?"

Ava pondered. "I suppose you may be right. I mean, he was her husband—he knew what she was like. What else has been nagging that overworked, suspicious brain of yours?"

"It's the eyes of the young man who accosted me a few days after Barbara died. He didn't look like he was approaching me to introduce himself. Luckily, Detective Jones stepped in. I was thinking about Bob Cole and his dealings with Joey. Who's to say Walter didn't have a hired gun of his own?"

Ava looked aghast. "Are you suggesting Walter paid someone to kill Barbara?"

I contemplated her question. "I don't know. It would certainly explain how they ended up being at the wrong place at the wrong time."

"Or," Ava emphasized, "if your theory is correct, being at the right place at the right time—for a murderous husband and his hired assassin, that is."

Bruce, who had become quiet, pulled the car over and parked. We were still at least three blocks from our destination. "I need to interrupt."

Ava looked from me to him. "What is it, Bruce? Did we get a flat tire?"

He shook his head. "No, but there is something I need to say before we reach the funeral home in about two minutes."

Ava and I listened. It wasn't often that he demanded the floor. He looked somber and focused. "I appreciate that you are trying to help out the police and solve this case, but I need you to remember why we're here today. It is not for an opportunity to observe suspects. It is to honor a woman whose life was cut short. That woman's husband, whom at this point we can only assume is innocent, will be burying his life partner. I am requesting that you both keep your sleuthing on hold during the funeral."

Ava kissed her husband on the cheek. "I'm sorry, hon."

"Me too," I said. "And you're right, Bruce. I'm sorry I got a little carried away. Now is not the time."

Bruce looked relieved. "Thank goodness. You are each allowed to resume suspicious theories in one hour."

Ava snapped her fingers and began to rifle through her purse. She pulled out a small glass bottle with a small stopper at the top and handed it to me. "I almost forgot about this. Here is your little perfume sample. I didn't get you a whole bottle since I know you're more of a Chanel

Number Five girl. I have one for you, Mary, and Jo."

"Oh, nice. Thanks!" I took the capped miniature bottle and opened it, dabbing my wrists and neck. The heady perfume quickly filled the car with its signature scent.

We arrived at the cemetery, where people were already beginning to gather. Bruce let us out and carried on to park the car, promising to catch up to us momentarily. Ava and I walked next to each other, both too interested in finding out who was there to bother with trivial conversation. I took a scan of the small crowd and spotted more than a few familiar faces. Walter Wiggins was the first one I noticed. He was coming out of the adjacent funeral parlor, looking grim, walking toward the group. He waved at someone, but the friendly gesture was not paired with a matching smile. I wondered who the recipient was of the formal, unwelcoming hello. I followed his line of sight. I felt no surprise to see Jane Humphries at the other end.

Jane returned Walter's wave with an equal lack of warmth. Her face was tighter than usual—a feat in itself. But instead of summarily dismissing it as cold and uncaring, as I might've done a week earlier, I paid more attention and detected what I guessed to be a hint of despair under its mask of apathy. Instead of the typical haughty smirk that usually crossed her face, the corners of her mouth were turned down, and I think her lips were trembling ever-so-slightly. While her eyes showed little emotion, her eyebrows were furrowed. The closer I came, the more certain I was that Jane was holding on by a thread. I felt sorry for her and wondered why she was so unwilling to show vulnerability, even at the most appropriate of moments. She was standing next to Joe, Sr., Joey, and Melanie, whose arm was linked with a dapper young man, whom I assumed must be her betrothed. Joe, Sr. and Jr. spoke to each other with hushed voices, and Melanie stayed close to her husband-to-be, the pair often gazing at each other, clearly having eyes for no one else.

Robin Manners was there, dressed in an exquisitely tailored black dress, standing next to Grant Marshall. While obviously in conversation, they rarely made eye contact, seemingly trying to look at anything other than each other, although both focused on what the other was saying. It didn't seem hostile but rather awkward, as if by looking at each other they were doing something wrong. He looked remarkably tired, much different than the celebratory mood he had clearly been in last time I saw him, when he was standing on a chair and raised a glass to me as I passed by the gentleman's room at Twin Oaks Country Club.

Just steps away now, I began to look out for Mary and Jo whom I guessed had to be among those milling about. I was certain I spotted a muted violet scarf belonging to Mary and was just about to call out to her when my view was blocked and all I could see was the tailored vest of a suit, suddenly within inches of my face. I looked up to see another familiar face before me, this one perhaps the most unexpected so far. Ava and I automatically grabbed each other's hands as we looked up to meet the intense gaze of Darryl Walker. Ava's old beau must've seen us before we saw him.

Ava drew in a long breath. "Well, if you aren't a sight for sore eyes." I could feel her instant tremble but she hid her nerves well with a bright and chipper voice.

"It's been a long time, Ava," Darryl said, with a hint of a smile.

"Yes, it has. I don't think I've seen you since high school."

Darryl's eyes cast over to me. The smile faded. "Hello, again, Izzy."

I flushed, not nearly as practiced as Ava for playing it cool, as she called it. "Hi, Darryl."

He looked back to Ava, unwilling to concede any personal space. "We had some good times, didn't we?"

Ava nodded. "We did. Hard to believe it's been fifteen years."

"Seems like a lifetime ago to me," Darryl said. "But you seem to remember every detail. I got a history lesson on my own life just the other day from—"

"Detective Jones!" I exclaimed, as the officer stepped out from behind our former classmate. I nearly shouted his name.

The detective didn't seem to mind. An amused smile stretched across his freshly shaven face as he looked at me then took in the scene before him. I wasn't sure if his suit was new or just pressed, but I couldn't help but notice the nice fit of the jacket around his broad shoulders. His natural ruggedness couldn't be scrubbed away but it was nice to see he could clean up when required. His presence seemed to cue Darryl to give us a little breathing room. He eyed Darryl with a less friendly manner.

"Have I interrupted something, Mr. Walker?"

Darryl shook his head but only glanced at the detective briefly. "No, Detective Jones. I was just reminiscing with my old classmates. Ladies, if you can spare a few minutes after the service, I'd appreciate it if you would come and find me."

Ava and I exchanged a looked then nodded, silently agreeing with one another to do just the opposite. He seemed satisfied with our misleading reply and faded back into the growing crowd. As Detective Jones began to ask us if we were okay, Bruce showed up and a bell rang to let people know the service was about to start. We walked over to where the funeral was being held. I spotted Mary and Jo across from us, on the other side of the casket. We waved at each other solemnly then waited for the service to begin.

We didn't have to wait long. Walter chose to have her burial and funeral service together, skipping the traditional requirement of pallbearers. The local clergyman, Reverend Calvin Moore, got up and began the service by introducing himself and thanking everyone for coming to the service for Barbara. Walter sat on a chair next to Jane, Joe, Sr., and Jr., and Melanie, plus her fiancé. There were a few others on chairs, but I didn't recognize their faces, and guessed they were out-of-town relatives. The rest of the community of Twin Oaks who had come out to pay respects stood behind the seated family members, including Mary and Jo, or on the other side of the casket, like me, Ava, Bruce, Detective Jones, and others. Because so many people showed up, unusual for a graveside funeral, everyone stood close together in order to see and hear the service.

It was getting warm outside, and although the sun mostly stayed behind some blessed clouds, it was obvious many people in the crowd were feeling the heat in their suits and formalwear. Reverend Moore seemed aware of the issue and tactfully seemed to move the service along at a speedy pace. Walter seemed despondent through most of the traditional speech. When asked to come up and say a few words about his beloved partner by the clergyman, Walter needed encouragement to the point of almost awkwardness, although in the end, he came through.

In what may have been the most uncomfortable few minutes of the day, Walter seemed to struggle to find kind words about his wife other than his mention of her tennis swing—a skill everyone present knew he had never actually witnessed. It became even worse as he attempted to show those in attendance a tearful good-bye to his wife, reaching out to touch the casket with one hand while covering his dry eyes with the other, all the while peeking over at the onlookers to make sure he was getting the attention he seemed to long for. It crossed my mind, as I looked on in horror, that if Twin Oaks ever began a drama club, Walter should have a pre-existing ban stemming directly from this performance. I watched Jane send virtual daggers from her eyes as the pathetic scene unfolded. Luckily, Reverend Moore hastily ended the moment, playing along with Walter's shenanigans, praising the showy concern, while quickly leading him away from center stage. Walter seemed pleased by the attention. He proceeded to strut over to a brand new convertible coupe, parked nearby. After revving the engine, he flung off his fedora, turned on an upbeat song, and drove away, whistling along to the catchy tune. He never looked back, to see the people left behind, their mouth gaping open in utter disbelief.

With the funeral ending on such a sudden and awkward moment, people seemed uncertain as to what to do next. Mary, a perpetual expert on social graces and a natural diplomat, made her way to the head of the confused gathering. It was clear she had something to offer but was struggling to gain the attention of the crowd to get her idea heard. Ava stepped out next to her and whistled louder than a male cicada searching for a mate. It silenced everyone immediately and drew attention to where they stood. Ava nodded silently and handed the floor to Mary, who then invited everyone to her estate for tea and sandwiches. With a good deal of the crowd looking interested, she then hustled to the funeral parlor and called home to warn her housekeeper. Luckily, Mary asked for a brief interlude to give herself time to get there first and help prepare her home for guests.

Jo went ahead with Mary. They were going to stop by our favorite bakery and pick up a variety of treats. Bruce, Ava, and I stopped off at their house on the way to drop off Bruce so he'd be around for the kids if they came home early from their outings with friends, and Ava quickly changed into a lighter, sleeveless summer dress in a muted pink cinched with a slim, black belt. I borrowed a sky-blue capped sleeve blouse that tucked in neatly to my pencil skirt. Feeling more relaxed, we bid Bruce goodbye and were on our way. We stopped to pick up a bouquet of flowers and a few hors d'oeuvres, consisting mostly of cheese, crackers, and deli meats.

By the time we arrived at Mary's, it looked like the somber mood of the funeral had lifted, and the whole thing had turned into more of a summer soiree. We also felt a little foolish thinking Mary and her amazing housekeeper, Mrs. Collins, wouldn't have everything completely under control. It looked like the gathering had been planned months in advance, considering the amount of food, drinks, and chairs that had been set up in what looked like perfectly organized fashion. Of course, upon seeing Mrs. Collins as we walked up the winding driveway, we could see the aura of the spontaneity had taken its toll on her.

We had known the older Scottish housekeeper for many years and were well aware of her rules and regulations regarding organization and event planning. No doubt the bull-like yet loveable lady was looking a little disheveled with her round cheeks even rosier than usual and her perfect bun, just a little unkempt. Her thick strong legs hustled around as we approached, and she barely acknowledged us as we bid her hello.

"Can we help out, Mrs. Collins?" I asked, feeling just slightly concerned at her shortness of breath.

She brushed back her stray hairs with a strong hand. "You two? Ha, I'd have to be hard pressed to have you lot help me out. I prefer you to stay mingling out here and away from my kitchen and pantry. Anything you need, ask before you go stomping about making a mess of my territory. And before you ask, ladies, the chardonnay is cooling on ice. Now, enough chit chat, be on your way and I'll be on mine."

"Yes, ma'am," we said in unison.

She rolled her eyes at us and chased us away with flapping hands. "Get, get," she demanded.

We followed instructions and headed straight toward the small crowd of people mingling about and enjoying the beautiful atmosphere provided by the sprawling oceanfront estate. Ava poured each of us a respectable glass of wine, and we began to walk toward our dear friend and hostess, where she smiled confidently and chatted up a small group of ladies.

Before we could reach them, we were cut off by the same figure who blocked the sun at the funeral—Darryl Walker stood in front of us, looking intently as if he had been waiting for us, yet again. It felt like déjà vu, and I was just about ready to lose my temper with the inappropriateness of the persistent former classmate I felt no need to see again. Ava seemed to feel the same way and while she said hello, it was with obvious less cheer in her voice.

Darryl held his hand up and asked us to please give him a minute of our time. We looked at each other. I gave a quick peek to make sure we were nowhere near the shore, then agreed to follow the intense man who seemed determined to have our attention.

He tried to smile as he led us toward an old oak tree.

"Thank you for giving me a few minutes of your time. I know this is not the ideal situation for a class reunion, but I'd like to bring you up to date with my life for a very specific reason."

We both smiled lightly. Ava cleared her throat. "Darryl, high school was a long time ago. We've both got our own families now, and we don't really focus on the past much anymore."

He looked disappointed. I put my hand on his arm as we walked. "You were a good guy then, and what happened to you was very unfortunate. The only reason I brought it up to Detective Jones was that I didn't want to seem like I was holding anything back in the search for a murderer. If it hurt you, I'm sorry."

Darryl pressed his lips together. "I appreciate you saying so. I was upset when the detective approached me about it, as if time was frozen and I was being punished again for disappointing my father. Up until an hour ago, I even thought I was going to be accused of killing Barbara and Bob Cole. But today luck was on my side."

I was confused. "I hope you don't mind my asking, but what changed today?"

"I saw the man who could prove where I was when Bob Cole was killed. When the police first questioned me, I couldn't remember his name. Then I spotted him at the funeral. Right after Barbara's husband left, I grabbed Detective Jones and told him. At first, I don't think he believed me. Then he went and asked the fellow. Since Detective Jones was convinced the murders were related, when I was able to provide a solid alibi for the second murder, he finally seemed to believe the truth. That I was innocent—of Bob Cole *and* Barbara's murder. Now I finally feel free to start my new beginning—right now, today. I feel like it's Barbara's way of apologizing for all the hurt she caused me years ago."

Ava smiled at him sympathetically. "And what does that mean for you, Darryl?"

"It means this," he said, as he led us to a shady area under an old tree, toward a pretty young woman, holding a young infant in her arms. "This is my wife, Polly, and my new son. When we found out Polly was pregnant, I knew it was the perfect time to return to Twin Oaks. I wanted to see you two because you were always kind and Polly doesn't know anyone here. I thought maybe you could be friends."

I felt the first genuine show of emotion as Darryl teared up.

"I'm sorry, I just never thought I'd be so blessed. They are my dream come true—and now my whole life."

His wife walked over to him and gave him a kiss. "You are the sweetest man I've ever met." Then she turned to us. "Hi there, Darryl had told me a lot about you two. I'm a little silly at times, you see. He said my sense of humor reminded him of you two." She reached out her hand. "I'm Polly and this is our new son, Josh."

Ava and I quickly recovered from our shock to welcome the new mother to our small community.

But if Darryl was innocent, who was left?

Before I had time to process the thought, a familiar face joined our little reunion party. Grant Marshall made his way over after he called out to Darryl from across the property. He jogged over with a huge grin on his face.

"Afternoon, ladies, Darryl, I know I shouldn't be all smiles right now. But from father to father, can we help it?" he said, looking at Darryl.

They exchanged an energetic handshake. Darryl shook his head. "Were your ears burning? Because we were just talking about you."

Before he could answer, Ava put up her hand. "I hate to interrupt, but why, may I ask do I smell the distinct scent of Shalimar on you? It's a lovely fragrance, of course, but I'm not used to smelling it on a gentleman."

Grant blushed. "You'll have to excuse the oddity of it. I'm afraid just when I was heading out the door to come to the service, my new bundle of joy had a rather unpleasant accident on my only pressed suit. My wife thought she had it out with a cloth, but when I picked up Robin from the shop, she nearly fell over from the stink. She had this little bottle of perfume and doused me in it."

"Oh good thinking, Robin, wherever you are," Ava stated.

"I dropped her off before coming here," Grant explained. "She finished everything she needed to do just in the nick of time to catch her flight."

"Flight?" I asked. "Where is she going?"

"She's going to Paris—in about three hours. It's been hard for her, all the baby stuff and the shop—I mean, that place was her life. She's going to re-invent herself in the city of lights. No doubt she'll do it, too. She always seems to land on her feet."

Darryl leaned in toward him and lowered his voice. "Has that appeased the wife? Now that the ex is out of your hair?"

Grant looked at Ava and me. We pretended not to hear. He just nodded at Darryl and let out a slow, long, exaggerated breath. "Anyways, I'd better be going. My wife and son are waiting for me at home."

"How old is your little one?" Ava asked.

"He's brand new, like Darryl's son. Darryl and I were at the hospital at the same time, you see. That's where we met."

Darryl grinned. "I brought my wife to the hospital, around sunrise, when her water broke. They told me to leave and come back in a few hours' time, when they were ready for me. It was too far to go home and nothing was open yet so I found an empty room and hid," Darryl said. "Luckily, Grant found me."

Grant chuckled. "I was in a similar situation—my wife was in labor—I was just a little more calm. I decided to head to the club and wait so I went into what I thought was an empty room to change and clean myself up. That's when I found Darryl—white as a ghost, poor guy. I made him come with me to the club while we waited for our wives to give birth."

"It was a much better idea than hiding out. In fact, it may have saved my life since it gave me a solid alibi."

"Glad to have helped," Grant said, slapping Darryl on the shoulder.

My mind raced. "Wait—I think I saw you that day— but that was hours after Bob Cole was found dead."

"Yes, and if I'm not mistaken, I was standing on a chair, with a beverage in my hand, doling out yet another cheers to uninterested fellow patrons, when you passed by me. Let's just say that was after a long morning of celebrating with my new friend here. By the time you saw me, poor Darryl was napping on a nearby sofa. Luckily, for all involved, we were soon roused by the hospital to return to our awaiting wives."

"Sounds like quite the morning," Ava said.

"From what I can remember," Darryl said. The men laughed.

"Anyways, good to see you all," Grant said. "Hopefully, next time, it'll be under better circumstances."

He left, and not long after, Darryl and his family did, too.

We finally found Mary and Jo sitting on lounge chairs, sipping wine, and talking over the day. By that time, it was just the four of us left.

"Pass me a bottle and a straw," Ava stated, flopping down next to Mary.

"I think I'll stick to water," I said quietly.

They all paused and looked at me with concern.

"Something's wrong and I feel like it's on the tip of my tongue," I explained. "I need to have my wits about me until I get out whatever it is my brain seems unable to unravel."

"It's probably just the stress of the day," Mary said, leaning over to pat my knee.

Jo seemed to agree. "That had to be one of the worst funeral's I've ever attended. I was standing behind Jane

Humphries and I could actually hear her gritting teeth during Walter's speech."

"Could it even be called a speech?" Ava demanded. "I tell you, if I go before Bruce, I will have a list of adjectives for him to memorize before the ceremony. I don't even think he mentioned love, although I suppose he sees it as until death do you part. I guess he figures he's free to do as he pleases now."

"I think he'd show more emotion if the club closed. No doubt that's where he headed after the funeral."

"If only he could've dedicated himself to his wife the way he did the club."

"Their level of commitment seemed fairly mutual, I must say. Although, I do believe they were ready to try again. I heard the ladies at the club discussing the Wiggins' plans when Barbara—"

"When Barbara was murdered," I said, sitting up straight. "Ava, we need to go. Now."

Before I finished talking, I was running to her car.

Ava cursed and took off her heels to catch up. "You'd better drive."

"Damn straight," I said, hopping in the driver's seat. She barely had the door closed when we peeled out of Mary's long, winding driveway.

"Where are we going?" she demanded.

"To the police station," I said. "We need help grounding a flight."

With my foot to the pedal, we arrived at the station in minutes. Detective Jones was at his desk, still in his fancy suit, reading through his notes.

He stood up when we ran in and met us at the front desk. "What is it?"

Chapter 31

R obin Manners sat in the back of the police cruiser looking angry when we spotted her from the window. She was then escorted into the station by a rookie constable, who seemed relieved to pass the stiff-armed lady over to Detective Jones for questioning.

"I just missed my flight," she said, her eyes flashing. "What is the meaning of this?"

Detective Jones led her into the station. She stopped when she saw Ava and me standing next to his desk. She looked less angry and more defeated when she realized we were there for her, too. She stopped pulling her arms away from the detective and slumped herself into a chair, looking nothing like the picture-perfect woman we were used to seeing.

"Finally figured it out, did you?" she said.

Ava covered her mouth. "Robin, tell me it's not true."

Robin looked up at the ceiling and a single tear ran down her cheek. "Barbara Wiggins. The woman I trusted who took my dream—my life—and threw it away to teach her husband a petty lesson."

Detective Jones barely had time to sit down before she continued. "You know I'm glad you got me before getting on that plane. I never even wanted to see Paris. I just wanted to get my poison away from Grant. He and his perfect little family deserve to be happy. He was good to me—unlike that selfish witch." She looked from Ava to me. "You've got to tell me, how did you figure it out?"

Detective Jones gave me the floor. I looked at her. "It was that day you were late for work, wasn't it? I saw you crying outside. You said it was because you found out Grant was going to be a father. But you already knew that, didn't you? You'd known for months, I'd guess, based on how close you and your ex-husband still were."

She nodded but didn't say a word.

I continued. "It was the shop—*your* baby—that had you upset. Grant told you the business was failing and you were heartbroken."

"That's right," Robin said. "But I didn't know I was going to kill Barbara—not then, at least. And I wouldn't have either, if she hadn't destroyed the business intentionally."

I pressed my lips together. "But when you realized she did it to get back at her husband, you decided to kill her."

She nodded. "It was as if fate handed me the weapon. I left the shop that night in a rage, realizing she had ruined any chance for me to get it back by making such a mess of the finances. Then fate took over—I saw Joey

Humphries hide the anchor, then I saw the Wiggins'
strolling along, not a care in the world. She was completely unaware or unconcerned that she had ruined everything I had worked my whole life for. I put everything
into that shop and she didn't give a damn. So I decided,
then and there, to show her I could be uncaring, too. I
could take away what she cared about most—herself."

Detective Jones leaned forward. "And Bob Cole?"

"That was easy. I asked him to meet me down near
Cooper's Bridge—before the shops were open. I pleaded
with him to reconsider letting me have my business back,
and reminded him how well it did under my ownership.
He laughed at me." She paused then smiled. "It was quite
satisfying to watch the smirk fade from his lips."

"And how did that come about?" the detective asked
calmly.

"Not quite as quickly as Barbara," Robin stated mat-
ter-of-factly. "The anchor was a far superior choice, to be
honest. I picked up a large rock and struck him when he
turned his back to leave. But without the height and
speed the bridge naturally provided, it took considerably
more effort on my part—not that I minded. That man required the smugness beaten out of him. And, like I said, I
was happy to oblige."

The detective signaled two uniformed officers to
come forward. They handcuffed Robin as Detective
Jones explained her rights. She was then led away quietly, her cruel words leaving both Ava and I at a loss for
anything more to say. When she was out of sight, the detective instructed us to go home, take a rest, and be pre-

pared to return later to answer some final questions regarding the case. Ava and I listened to the instructions and left the building, mumbling our thanks to Detective Jones and continuing to look at one another for reassurance that the other was okay.

Mary and Jo had been awaiting our return anxiously. They were even in the same lounge chairs where we had left them earlier, only now they were armed with heaps of sandwiches and cookies ready for us to devour, at the insistence of the housekeeper, our beloved Mrs. Collins. We happily obliged then shared the unfortunate series of events that led to the back-to-back murders.

For a while afterward, we all just sat on the lounge chairs, arranged side-by-side, each looking out toward the ocean. The resonant crashing of waves coming into shore was calming and gave us time and space to nurture our wounded spirits, while allowing the misty salt spray to refresh our worn nerves. We must've sat there for hours, no one feeling the need to discuss the ugly truth of what happened, allowing each of us to process it on our own, enjoying the unspoken camaraderie only years of friendship can provide.

Ava took a break to call Bruce and tell him what happened. He told her to take whatever time she needed and to come home when she was ready, knowing full well it would likely be well into the wee hours of the morning. She shared a rare moment of humble gratitude with us for having such a wonderful husband, a tenderness we knew she always felt but rarely spoke of.

It sparked the beginning of a round table discussion

of gratitude, one we were all ready to embrace. We each discussed the many things in our lives we were thankful for, ending with a surprise attack on the unsuspecting Mrs. Collins, all of us wrapping our arms around her as she shooed us away, trying not to succumb to the uncouth giggle we could see hiding just below her pursed lips and swatting hands.

Twin Oaks got back to its everyday life within a week or two. The tears shed for the departed dried up quicker than most would want to admit. But there was a kindness sparked throughout our town that signaled an awareness of lessons learned too late. It was gratefulness for life, for forgiveness, and for kindness to those around each other.

My nearly grown children returned from camp and seemed pleased by my energetic attitude and renewed interest in the family business. My son shyly admitted he hoped to take over the business just as soon as he could and my daughter began to ask about college in New York.

I felt ready to take on the world again, with my kids by my side and my friends in my court. It was time to come out from the shadows of grief and allow the light be my guide. Tragedy would serve as a lesson for me, and I was ready to accept and embrace whatever would come my way.

About the Author

Lynn McPherson grew up in various parts of Canada, from the Canadian Rockies to the big city of Toronto. Travel was always a part of her life, starting with a trip to Europe at the curious age of two. Many moons later, Lynn's love of adventure and exploration never ceased, eventually leading her to the exciting world of writing, where she is free to go anywhere, anytime. Having a particular love of New England, possibly stemming from a snowy winter's night spent at a cozy inn, Lynn has always known this is where her mystery series must take place. She is a member of the *International Thriller Writers* and *Sisters in Crime*.